A BETTER ENGAGEMENT

A BLUEBIRD SKY NOVELLA

ELLORY DOUGLAS

Copyright © 2024 by Ellory Douglas

1. FICTION, ROMANCE, CONTEMPORARY

Trade paperback 978-1-7383011-4-0

Ebook 978-1-7383011-5-7

All rights reserved.

No part of this book may be reproduced in any form or by any electronic or mechanical means, including information storage and retrieval systems, without written permission from the author, except for the use of brief quotations in a book review.

This is a work of fiction. Names, characters, places and incidents either are the product of the author's imagination or are used fictitiously, and any resemblance to actual persons, living or dead, business establishments, events or locales is entirely coincidental.

❦ Created with Vellum

For everyone who loves uncomplicated sweetness, I wanted to give you a treat.
So, here's a delicious cream pie.

Along with some just desserts.

AUTHOR'S NOTE

A BETTER ENGAGEMENT IS AN EXTENDED EPILOGUE TO A BETTER Proposal. It can be read as a stand alone novella, but you'll get all the inside jokes and context if you read A Better Proposal first.

If you don't have a copy handy or need a refresher, here's what you need to know.

- Jill and Alex meet at university, where he was the tyrannical teacher's assistant who made her first year chemistry class unbearable.
- Eight years later, Jill gets out of an abusive relationship and moves across the country for a fresh start.
- Alex and his best friend and business partner, Nick, hire her to write a funding (one might say, a *better*) proposal for their start up company.
- Alex melts her frosty exterior and, ah, helps her find her voice.
- Everything goes to shit when Nick submits inflated result projections to the government. It looks like *Alex* had submitted the results in such a way that Jill thought Alex used and betrayed her.

- HEARTACHE! PINING!
- An internal investigation reveals the truth.

Chapter 1 - With This Ring takes place three months after Chapter 27 of A Better Proposal.

Chapter 2 - Favourite picks up the morning of the Epilogue of A Better Proposal.

Chapter 13 - Lines takes place during Chapter 29 of A Lucky Shot.

1

WITH THIS RING

"Do you think she'll like me?" Jill asks for the millionth time, her teeth worrying at her lower lip. "I mean, I've been practicing my French and I can say a couple of things, but what if she asks me about anything other than my favourite colours or to sing a Christmas carol—"

I pause in fastening the buttons of my shirt. Jill is making me dizzy with her pacing a narrow strip in the old bedroom that was my home in university.

"Bean." I catch her hand as she paces by, and smooth my hands down her arms. "She's going to love you."

"Do you think?"

The out-sized, hopeful expression on her face melts my heart. If only she knew. Growing up with the family she did, she still can't believe that we like each other, that there's so many of us, and that we don't lie awake at night panicking before we see each other next. She wants to be accepted into it so bad she's twisted herself into a knot of Gordian complexity with worry.

Besides my mom and my sister, Jill is essentially meeting my entire maternal family all at once. Four generations are packed under one roof in a Montreal suburb, with more coming tomorrow. It's my grandmother's first Christmas without her husband. None of us wanted her to be alone for it.

It also means there are over a dozen people staying in this three-bedroom bungalow. If I didn't love everyone between these walls so much, I'd be crawling out of my skin to get some peace and quiet.

The open bedroom door lets in a muffled mixture of French and English wafting through the halls. At least we have a bedroom door. Jill and I lucked out, and won the draw for my old room. Sure, the bed is small, but we could be stuck sleeping on an air mattress in the living room. My sister, her wife, and their sons get that honour.

If a recent sleepover is any indication, there is a one-hundred percent chance those two boisterous toddlers will barrel their way into our bed tomorrow morning, and a ninety-percent chance I'm being woken up with an accidental kick to the nuts. Again.

I pull my girlfriend into my lap and wrap my arms around her until her rapid respiration slows to match my own.

"My mom loves you. My dad loves you. Gem and Bea and Jake and Henry all love you," I say, nuzzling her neck. "But the reason I'm sure mémé will love you is that you make me happy, and that's all she's ever wanted for her grandkids."

A half-smile twists her mouth, and she gives a determined nod. She drops a kiss on me before fastening the last of the buttons of my shirt. "Let's go meet grand-maman."

No way I'm correcting her accent now.

We're stopped no less than six times on the way to the kitchen, accosted by cousins and aunts and uncles in a barrage of introductions that leaves Jill wide-eyed and smiling mutely.

After my uncle improvises a poem in French, bending the pronunciation of Jill's name to rhyme with *fille* and *ville* and *gentille*, I lean in to whisper, "Don't worry. I'll remind you of everyone's names later."

Mémé's eyes light up as she sees me and waves us over from

her perch, surrounded by dishes of food and a gaggle of descendants.

"*Crevette!*" Her old nickname for me garners snickers from a cousin within earshot.

Still her shrimp, after all these years.

As soon as we are within reach, she puts her hand on my arm to help herself down from her chair and pulls me into a surprisingly firm hug. Not like she's ever been tall, but the top of her head doesn't even reach my collarbones anymore. A fleeting glimpse of my mother looking like that one day flashes across my mind.

It's been too long.

I blink back the moisture pooling behind my eyelids and return the hug. Short, yes, but she's not nearly as frail looking as I feared she might be, voice strong and eyes bright, if not a little rheumy.

She's already turning to my timid-looking girlfriend and planting kisses on both of her cheeks. "And this is Jill," she declares in rapid French, a huge smile spread across her wrinkled skin. "It is such a pleasure to meet my Alexandre's girl!"

Jill looks like a deer in the headlights, trying to sift through the few words she knows to translate my grandmother's greeting. "Um, *je suis si heureuse de votre rencontrer, Madame Pelletier,*" she says in her best halting French. "*Ton,* I mean, *votre petit-fils est un très bon cuisinier.*"

My grandmother's eyes crinkle at the corners, and she switches to English. "I'm pleased to meet you, too. You must call me mémé, like all the kids," she says to Jill, and then to me in French again, "See, I told you those cooking lessons would pay off."

Here I'd thought her forcing me to learn to cook had been her attempt to make me a fully functioning adult. Turns out she'd been a prescient wingwoman.

Smart woman, my mémé.

She takes Jill by the elbow and steers her to the dining room.

"Come," she says in English again. "You will sit with me at dinner."

"Try and save me a seat on the other side," I say, but I get the sense that either my cousin's daughter or Jake or Henry is going to claim that spot.

Jill always said she wanted family. She's stuck with an entire clan, now.

After third helpings of dinner have been eaten and the dishes have been cleared, a few of the kids pull Jill from the table.

My grandmother waves me over to take over Jill's vacated seat. "Your girl is very pretty."

I catch a glimpse of Jill's piggy-backing my cousin's daughter through the living room. The little girl is pointing at random household objects and making Jill repeat everything back in French. Jake and Henry bounce at Jill's heels, shouting the words in English at their French cousin. Jill must feel my eyes on her. When she looks up and meets my gaze, her smile detonates a bomb in my chest, and for a moment, I forget to breathe.

"She is the most beautiful thing I've seen in my life," I manage to say, finally.

"She loves you."

I can't stop the smile that curves my mouth. "Yes."

"You love her."

"I do."

"You're going to marry her." It isn't a question.

From the moment Jill first smiled at me, I was hers. Our first kiss was a dream. The first time we made love was bliss. Hearing her say *I love you* the first time made me complete.

The month we were apart felt like a black hole had been punched into my soul.

Jill still hasn't forgiven herself for not coming to me first, even if it could have gotten her fired. I keep wondering if I had cancelled my road trip, would we have found the changes together? Could we have avoided the pain of the investigation altogether? Hindsight is twenty-twenty, but if we spend our time regretting the choices we made in the past, we'll never have a future.

The three months she's been in my arms again have been the best of my life. I don't plan on letting her go again.

My future is her. As soon as she's ready.

"We've only been together for six months," I hedge.

"Alexandre, you have never brought a girl home to meet the family." Mémé pats my cheek with a wrinkled hand. "You know yourself. You know your heart. You're going to marry her."

It's like she can see directly into my brain. I nod, and work my smile around the lump in my throat. "As soon as she'll let me."

"Good boy." She pulls her engagement ring over an arthritic knuckle, leaving only the gold wedding band on her finger. "I'll give this to you now."

Stunned, I stare at the ring resting in my palm. For sixty-four years, this ring sat on my grandmother's finger. The silver band curves around a small sapphire, the prongs thinned by a lifetime of wear. It's nothing like the flashy diamonds dominating hands now. Sixty-four years with Jill would be a dream. Even that wouldn't be enough time.

I don't know anything about carats or cuts or anything. But this ring, with a lifetime of history in my hand, feels *so right*.

"Are you sure?" I croak out.

"I said yes to your grandfather when he asked me with this ring. She'll say yes to you."

"Thank you," I whisper, clutching the ring. I catch Jill's eye from the other room, I want to drop to my knee in front of her right now.

Not in front of a crowd. No surprises. Don't rush her. I swallow hard. "She's not ready yet. She needs time."

"I didn't mean right now, *Crevette*," my grandmother says, grinning. "You'll know when the time is right."

Jill is holding my gaze from the other room, bending over to whisper in the ears of the kids who are hanging off of her. Henry peels away from the group to rush into the kitchen, wrapping his arm around my thigh.

"Jilly says we can build snow forts tomorrow after presents!" he squeals, slipping between French and English. "Me and Jake are going to be on her team!"

This beautiful woman, who made my family fall in love with her almost as much as I do, gives me a look so guileless that an angel would seem nefarious beside her.

I know that look. Tomorrow morning, I'm getting a handful of snow shoved down my pants when she thinks I'm not looking.

Joke's on her. I never take my eyes off her.

I haul my nephew onto my lap, and wink at my grandmother. "Three against one sounds fair."

Now I need to watch for the perfect time to ask her the question I've been holding back on since I had her in my arms again. But the time has to be right. Too soon, and I'll scare her away again. She has to be ready first.

Good thing I'm a patient man. I can wait as long as it takes.

2

FAVOURITE

A year and two months later

"I love you, I love you."

A coffee cup clinks on the bedside table, and hands brace against my chest a moment later. The shiver that runs over my torso is partly from her cold hands. Mostly it's from the second, third, and fourth kisses that she feathers on my eyelids, jawline, and lips.

Every day I wake into the most beautiful dream. Those words, kisses, glorious coffee. In that order. Then, if I'm lucky, snuggles for as long as I can keep her in bed.

Some mornings, I hear her puttering around the house as I swim to the surface of consciousness. Other times, her lips on mine are the first thing I feel, and the words *I love you. I love you.*

It is my favourite way to wake up.

She slides under the covers beside me, tucks a freezing hand around my bicep, and nuzzles into my shoulder. "Good morning."

"Morning." My voice is froggy with sleep.

I have no idea what time it is. Barely know what day it is. All

I know is that she agreed to take a week off of work and I don't have to let her out of bed yet.

Muscle memory takes over, and I grab a handful of her ass. Her soft skin erupts into goosebumps under my palm as she shifts her hips against my thigh, and two things become apparent.

The first is that my girlfriend is not wearing underwear, and the second is that her hand is sneaking towards my groin.

I haven't even opened my eyes today and I'm already smiling. "Don't you have a run planned for this morning?" I tease.

"Actually ..." Her fist closes around my morning wood, and I hiss out a breath as she squeezes me down to my base. "What if I said I had some other cardio in mind?"

Damn. I take back what I said a minute ago. *This* is my favourite way to wake up.

Before I can crack my eyelids, she crawls on top of me, sliding her centre along the length of my cock with the most delicious rolls of her hips.

"Oh, fuck me," I whisper.

"That's the idea."

She's so wet for me already. I slip my hand between her thighs and thumb her clit in lazy circles, and fuck if I'm not aching to be inside her.

"Are you sure you don't want coffee first?" she whispers, breath hitching as I part her folds with my finger and notch myself at her entrance. "You seem s—"

The rest of her sentence is cut off with a sharp intake of breath as I slide in that first inch. I settle my hands over the flare of her hips, rock into her a few times, and let out a low groan. My entire body snaps into focus, all on the gorgeous woman on top of me. Her fingertips rake my chest, thighs already starting to quiver, and I'm still only halfway inside her.

"Just a little more," I coax. Goddamn, the way her heat envelopes me has me curling my toes. I guide her lower, easing her down, until I'm fully seated inside her. "*Fuck*, you take me so well."

"Because your cock is made for me."

Her teeth bite down on her lower lip as she cants her hips forward and picks up her pace. She's bathed in sunlight, glowing. Her tits bounce, half-hidden behind her sleep-mussed hair spilling over her shoulders, and the second I brush the pads of my thumbs over her rosy nipples, she loses control. Her wet heat clamps down on my cock as her orgasm ripples over her, my name fading into a moan that almost sounds painful.

It's music.

Before her body goes limp, I flip her onto her back with a *whoosh*. She's in no state to resist. Not like she ever does. The minute I figured out she likes it when I throw her around a little, I made a point to do it every day.

Easy enough. The meatheads I play against in rugby have a hundred pounds on her. And damn if I don't live for the giggly shriek she lets out every time I sweep her off her feet.

Or onto her back. I'm not picky.

I've got her folded in half with her ankles slung over my shoulders. She looks so good, loose-limbed and sated under me, I have to slow down, take her in.

"Alex, please." The way she's looking at me, *begging* me to unleash on her.

Fuck, this isn't going to take long.

I pump into her, over and over, until she's shaking again. When the last shudders leave her body, I let go. My blood is a dull roar in my ears, and my entire core winds tighter, tighter, until I explode, filling her up. The whole time she clings to me, fingers grasping my biceps, her breath ragged against my cheek.

Neither of us move as the pounding of my heartbeat fills my ears. I'm still inside her, feeling myself softening after our shared release. I push up onto an elbow, and trail kisses down her neck.

No lips yet. I'll spare her my morning breath. Plus, the little gasps she lets out when I attack her neck make me *feral*.

"Stop it!" she shrieks, shivering.

If I let her scream any longer, a giant pitbull will launch herself into bed in a heartbeat to rescue her favourite human. I halt my attack and wipe a hand over my face. Steam still rises in lazy tendrils from the cups she put on the nightstand before returning to bed to wake me up. It couldn't have been ten minutes ago.

God, I love morning quickies.

"Ready for coffee?" I ask with a grin, and hand her a cup before I tear myself away to grab her a washcloth.

I brush my teeth at lightning speed before staggering back to bed to pass her a cloth. She's up a second later and I watch her butt as she darts to the bathroom.

"Nice view," I call to her.

"You're welcome!" she sings back to me.

No doubt, I am a thankful man.

It would be too easy to fall back asleep, so I sit up and take my first swallows of coffee and try to focus on our day off together.

What I'm not going to do is think about being on the road the week after.

Even though I travel less now, it sucks more. No *I love you* alarm to start my day. Sure, we'll video chat every night and text good morning, at least on the days I'm in cell range, but it isn't the same.

I'm not nearly as busy as I was when we first met, and damn if it isn't great to not work eighty-hour weeks anymore.

I have staff now. Someone takes care of my accounting and filing. A contractor takes care of sites up north. I still need to deal with the ones down here. I still don't have anyone who can evaluate new sites.

Environmental remediation is pretty niche, and using my technology made it ... nicher. No one besides Nick could grasp what I had developed. But with the grant money Jill won us, I can train someone. Eventually.

Money isn't everything, but it solves a lot of problems.

But not all of them.

I only have one real problem outside of work. Not a *problem*. More like a question. I know what the answer will be, as long as I ask the right way and at the right time.

The ring has burned a hole in my nightside for over a year. A few times over the past couple months, it's felt almost right. But it needs to be absolutely, one-hundred percent perfect. I can't screw this up.

Jill drops into bed beside me and I snake out an arm around her middle to pull her under the covers again.

"What do you want to do today?" she asks.

I prop myself up enough to sip without sloshing my coffee. "Have a few ideas," I say, and pat the bed to signal Daisy's permission to join the snugglefest. "As soon as I finish cleaning up after Jake and Henry."

"The boys are getting so big," she says, burrowing deeper into the crook of my shoulder. Her tone is light, less brisk than her usual morning, ready-for-the-day chipperness. "I had a lot of fun this weekend."

It had been a great weekend. My sister, Gemma, dropped off my nephews for a two-night sleepover so she and Bea could get away. Jake has a crush on a girl in his class and Henry has a crush on their teacher. Both were already talking about kindergarten in the fall. They had meltdowns when they left, not sure if they were happier to see their moms or sad to be leaving Uncle Sandy and Auntie Jilly.

I take another swig of coffee, and chuckle. "Could have skipped the knee to the balls yesterday when Jake crawled into bed. Not sure how many more of those I can take before it makes having kids of our own a challenge."

"Funny you should say that," she starts, voice barely above a whisper, "can I ask you something?"

"Anything."

"It's been a few months since we've talked about kids."

I go still. I try not to bring up us having a baby too often. The last time was the day after my rugby team's Christmas party.

December twenty-second, to be exact.

Do we want them? Yes.

How many? Two (her) or three (me).

When ... she hasn't said.

She isn't even thirty yet. She's just been promoted. I can't rush her.

The first time I asked her if she wanted kids, we'd barely been dating a month. Even then I held off asking her for weeks. But when Dan dropped pictures of his newborn daughter in my team's group chat, the question fell out of my mouth before I could stop it.

And that had been too soon. The look in her eyes had been half-excitement, but the half-fear lurking underneath scared me as much as it scared her. Since then, I've waited for her to initiate every step in our relationship.

But if she's bringing it up now ...

"It has," I say, carefully. *Patience.*

"I have a physical in the fall."

"Two weeks after mine, right?" *Wait for it.*

She's drawing hearts with her fingertips on my bare stomach. "When do you want to have kids?"

"As soon as you'll give them to me," I blurt out, and suck in a breath.

So much for patience.

Quiet excitement and tentative hope pour out of her. "What do you think about me taking out my IUD?"

My heart stops in my throat. I'd have pulled the goalie a year ago. Hell, I'd drive her to her doctor to yank the thing right now. "You're ready to start our family?" I ask, hardly daring to breathe.

She pulls back to turn her brilliant grey eyes on me and nods.

Yes. The time is right.

Today. *Finally.*

I squeeze her closer and don't guard the smile that consumes my features.

"I think that's so perfect. So perfect."

She exhales, all minty and fresh on my neck, and whispers, "Okay."

Her smile is pressing against my skin and my heart is going to burst through my chest. "Today, you pick. Anything you want to do, whatever makes you the happiest, we'll do it."

"Even going to the plant store?"

I kiss her forehead. "Bean, I will buy you all the plants you want to kill."

I have never been happier that the plant store was closed.

Her second pick is our hike. An old favourite trail of mine that I took her on last summer. It quickly became our go-to escape. Off the beaten path, far enough away to not be crowded, and astonishing views at the top, where the world spreads around us in all directions.

The tail end of the winter's snow is packed hard underfoot, but the Chinook winds that blew in overnight left the air dry and warm. Almost tee shirt weather, even in the mountains.

For me, anyway. Jill is zippered into her worn cornflower blue hoodie that makes her glow, and more than once on the two hours up the trail I thought about pulling her into the treeline for a caress.

I give in, a couple times.

She stops to snug the laces on her hiking boots, scanning the path ahead of us before turning her smile on me again. It lights me up like the sun every time. So at peace, so happy, and my heart stops in my throat.

Now.

I've thought about this moment a thousand times. The right

words, the right place, but everything I practiced saying crowds on the tip of my tongue.

"It was two years ago today we met," I stammer.

"We met ten years ago," she corrects, and dodges my half-hearted attempt to swat her butt.

A nervous chuckle huffs from my throat. I've barely started and my voice is already shaking. "You know what I mean."

"I remember. Vividly." She pulls me in for a light kiss, tracing her fingers along my jaw. With how hard my heart is pounding right now, she must feel my pulse bouncing under her fingers, and she tilts her face to me in concern. "What's up?"

"You know, you never finished what you started."

Her nose scrunches in confusion. "What didn't I finish?"

"I hired you to do a job. You did half of it."

She grins. "Pretty well, too." The grant money her consultation won us helped my business achieve more in the last two years than I ever dreamed possible. All because of her. But that's not what I'm here for now.

"Amazingly well." I swallow hard. "But you never did help with my proposal."

Her teasing fades, and dawning realization sweeps her beautiful features. Her chest hitches as she draws breath, and her smile blossoms. "I didn't."

"Not sure I need help with this one, but I need to see if my partner is on board."

The ring has pressed like a brand into my thigh for the last two hours. I slip my hand into my pocket and wrap my fingers around it.

Her gaze flicks down as I pull my still-closed fist out of my pocket, and her eyes shine up at me. "Yes," she breathes.

"Are you ready for me to ask?"

"Yes," she says, louder, dancing on the spot.

"You're sure?" I can't help it. I want to draw out this moment as long as I can. Her face is glowing, the shiver of excitement running over her, and I want this to last forever. "I don't want to rush you—"

"Oh my god, Alex! Yes!" Jill screams into the valley and launches herself at me, wrapping her legs around my torso and clutching her hands to the sides of my face. Our lips find each other, a wild frenzy of kisses until Daisy's barking makes us stop.

Jill brushes the hair that escaped my toque under the brim, laughing and sniffing, and I lower her feet to the ground to wipe the happy tears from her cheeks.

I tilt my forehead to hers, eyes closed as I wrap my arms around her. Even through our clothes, I feel her heart pounding against mine, and I inhale shampoo and sweat and the sweet scent of the woman who just agreed to be my wife.

I sigh into her hair. "Just making sure."

I take her left hand to slide the ring on her finger, her right hand pressing to her mouth to hold back the giddy laugh that spills out.

It looks perfect on her. Anything would look perfect on her. She holds it out, fingers extended, and her mouth opens into an *O*.

"Alex," she whispers, "where did you get this?"

All of a sudden I worry it's not right. It's old-fashioned. It's small. It's not a diamond.

"It was Mémé's," I explain in a rush. "She gave it to me at Christmas for you, but we'll get something you want, anything you want. As long as you're happy."

"No." Tears mist her eyes. "This couldn't be more perfect. I love it so much. I love you so much."

I turn her hand to kiss her palm before I pull up straight with a jerk. All that practice, and I still forgot one thing. "Wait, I haven't actually asked yet. I need to do this right."

She buries her face in her hands, the sapphire scattering the sun's rays. "Okay, ask."

"Jill, my sweetness. From the first time you smiled at me I

knew I was going to love you for the rest of my life. You bring me joy I never thought possible. Every minute we are together is better than the one before, and I want to spend our lives together." I drop to my knee and look at the ring already on her finger. "I kind of did this out of order—"

"That's okay," she says, eyes shining, waving her hand.

I chuff a laugh. "Will you marry me?"

A fresh wave of tears fill her eyes, and she sobs into my neck again. "Yes, I'll marry you."

Yes. She said yes. She's going to be my wife.

I pull her close, burying my face in her hike-mussed hair. "You've made me the happiest man in the world."

Now, the minor detail of planning a wedding.

My control-obsessed Jillybean is going to be in her element.

3

ANXIETIES

Months engaged: *one*
Months to doctor's appointment: *seven*
Months until wedding: *unknown*

Someone should have given me a heads up to keep earplugs on hand for the next month.

We tell my mom and my sister first. When Jill held up her left hand to the FaceTime call, my grandmother's ring sparkling on her finger, my mom sobbed more than when I got my PhD. Gemma made Jill promise to call the minute I gave her any of, and I quote, "my little brother's usual bullshit," without actually declaring what that was. Even my nephews took it in stride that us getting married meant that neither of them would get to marry Auntie Jilly.

Sophie, in all her prescience, knew why we were calling before she answered, already screaming when the call connected. Which meant by the time we added Kyle to the call, she already texted him. With what Kyle's opinion of me used to be, it put me at ease to see him so happy for us.

All it took was two years of me treating his best friend right to earn his forgiveness.

The news blew up my rugby team's group chat for days. Half my team suggested to Jill it wasn't too late to change her mind, and the other half put a standing offer in to rescue her if I was holding her against her will. Clowns.

Even my emotionally-constipated dad got choked up when we called him.

But the high from telling the people we love over the last month has evaporated. Now, Jill is staring at the phone as if it's going to bite her.

Stealing herself to tell her parents we're engaged is like preparing to break the news of a terminal diagnosis.

Granted, the handful of conversations she's had with them in the last several months each spanned less time than it takes me to make an omelette. I timed it once, taking out the eggs from the fridge when Jill hit the call button, and sliding the plated omelette in front of her after her head had been resting on her folded arms a full minute after the call had ended. Not that she could eat it after.

I rub her back as she stares at her phone. "Are you sure you want to do this now?"

"Yes. I promised myself I'd do it as soon as I got back from Vancouver." She rubs at the space between her brows. "I can do this."

"But you're not doing it alone," I remind her, smoothing the hair away from her cheek and sliding the phone over to her. "We're calling them together."

Her shoulders unwind from her ears. "Oh, right," she says, and gives me a relieved smile. "You take such good care of me."

The caveman inside me puffs out his chest. Sitting beside her and holding her hand while she makes a phone call is easy. I will put my body between her and whatever would bring her harm.

Even if it's between her and the people who are supposed to love her beyond anything.

"We take care of each other," I say, kissing her temple and pulling her onto my lap. We always feel better when we're touching, like we draw on each other's energy. Sometimes she's giving it to me, sometimes I'm giving it to her. But it always balances. I squeeze her hand. "Do you want to rehearse anything?"

She sighs. "No. I'll just come out with it. No wait. Follow my lead? Maybe I'll say we've been talking about it for months, and …" She shakes her head. "No, I don't want to make something up. I could—"

"Or I can say I finally wore you down."

She clicks her tongue, but I can feel her smiling as some of the tension releases from her posture. "Okay, here goes everything."

The call connects on the first ring and her father's timid face fills the screen.

"My Jillian," he cries. "You look beautiful, my dear. Let me get your mother for you."

"Actually, we'd like to talk to you both, if you can stay on the video with her?" Jill's voice clips at the edges, like saying the words faster will make it easier.

This should be a joyous call. Their only child is getting married. Instead Jill is as tense as if she's confessing to totalling the family car instead of announcing an engagement.

Don't get me wrong. I'm a pain in the ass. I work too much. I leave my socks balled up in the laundry basket, and Jill has to tell me our plans start half an hour early if we need to get anywhere on time.

But I'm a business owner, with a PhD. In her mother's field, no less. Thanks to their daughter, my business has pulled in enough funding that was able to draw enough salary over the last couple years to fully pay off my student loans.

Gainfully self-employed, well-educated, and debt-free. And we *get* each other. We share the same values and want the same things in life. But most important is that their daughter feels safe with me. Like she can finally be herself.

You'd think that would make her parents happy. But I'm not

the one they—or rather, her mother—thought their daughter would end up with, and that has been unforgivable.

Although we've spoken on the phone a few times, I haven't met either Arnold or Lizanne in person as their daughter's boyfriend. I've seen her mother at conventions over the years, though ironically nothing in the past three, since my business has kept me too busy to travel. My staff is great, but they aren't Nick. Now that he isn't here to help shoulder the weight, my time away from the office is preciously guarded.

"Hi Mom, how are—"

"Jillian, so nice to *finally* hear from you again." Her mother turns her simpering smile to her husband, an overly quizzical knot between her eyebrows, "It's been so long I can't remember the last time you spoke to us."

"I called you on Christmas day, and hung up when you said it looked like I put on weight."

Not the start either of us would have hoped for, but Jill didn't back down from her mother's jab. Her therapist would tell her to cut the call there, but we are calling for a reason.

Jill's hand slides into mine, under the table and out of view. "We have some news. Alex and I are getting married."

A beat of silence echoes, and for a moment, I think they aren't going to say anything.

Her father breaks first. "Oh, that's wonderful!" He sounds like he means it, eyes shining and genuine smile consuming his features. He casts a glance to his wife, who looks like she is calculating the best response.

When it comes, it shouldn't surprise me, but it does. She lets out a shriek, and Jill jolts back into my chest.

"My baby is getting married?" Her mother clasps a flapping hand to her mouth, and hugs her husband with the other arm. "When? How? Tell me everything!"

A smile flutters at the corner of Jill's mouth. "You're really happy?"

"Honestly, Jillian. Of course. I'm overjoyed. We're ecstatic."

Both heads bob from the other side of the country. "You're our daughter. All we've ever wanted is for you to have the best life. Are you already planning? You must have it here in Toronto. We're paying for everything, of course," her mother says blithely, hand waving in loose circles. "We'll have to—"

"We haven't started planning anything," Jill cuts in. "We're going to enjoy being engaged for a while and figure out details later."

We're going to enjoy being engaged for a while. How long is a while? The space around my heart contracts, but years of people, not least of all the one on the other end of this phone call, pushing her to do things she isn't ready for made her default reaction to pressure to either freeze or run.

She's run from me once, fighting against the self-doubt and fear planted by her mother and ex.

I don't need more time. I would get married this afternoon, but I'll make sure Jill gets all the time she needs.

So instead, I swallow, and nod. "That's very generous," I say, not committing to anything without first discussing it with Jill. I add honestly, "Your daughter has made me the happiest man in the world."

"Oh, you." Lizanne wipes at her eye. Her father's eyes are misty, but I would swear her mother's are drier than a nun's liquor cabinet.

There's that act again.

A few minutes later, Jill ends the call and turns to me with a wary expression. "That was …"

"A whole lot better than we thought it would be?" I offer. "I'm proud of you."

She shrugs. "I feel like I built that up over nothing."

Not for the first time, I simmer at the thought of her family putting her in a position that sharing joy in life feels like a burden. I wonder what it will be like when, one day, we tell them that we are expecting a baby.

My heart catches in my throat. Her doctor's appointment

isn't for months, but if we get pregnant as soon as her IUD is removed, we could have a newborn as early as next fall. My arms tighten around her instinctively as visions of our baby at our wedding swarm my thoughts.

"What you said on the phone," I start carefully, "do you want a long engagement?"

She chews her thumbnail, then shakes her head. "No, but I don't want to rush planning, either. I want everything to be perfect."

Of course she does. I smile as I blow out a steady breath. "We'll take it one day at a time."

We can figure out the details as they come. As long as it makes her happy.

4

HOPE

Months engaged: *three*
Months to doctor's appointment: *five*
Months until wedding: *unknown*

IF I DON'T KICK DAISY OFF MY LEGS IN THE NEXT TWO MINUTES, I'M going to lose them to lack of circulation.

The light from the laptop resting on my thighs casts a faint glow, steadily dimming as my battery dwindles. I should shut down, anyway. Between me with my client load and Jill with the wedding planning—or *dreaming*, as she calls it—the last three months we've broken the *no screens in the bedroom* rule more and more. I set my laptop on the nightstand and try to shuffle Daisy to a more comfortable position, which earns me a doleful look.

Like she doesn't have a perfectly good dog bed three feet away.

"Spoiled brat." I scritch her under her chin. Daisy gives me a deep woof and settles her head between her paws.

Jill narrows her eyes at me, looking up from her own laptop perched on her crossed legs. "You better not be insulting my dog."

"Not an insult to state facts," I retort, but her attention is already back to the four tabs with nearly identical cake designs from local bakeries flashing across the screen.

Wedding planning apps didn't hold a candle to Jill's meticulous organization. She's already uninstalled the three trackers she downloaded. In their place are lists and spreadsheets and whiteboards. And Pinterest boards. And vision boards. So many boards.

For a brief moment, when we considered having a country farm-themed wedding, we even had chalkboards. Travis, the volunteer coordinator at the animal shelter who's turned into her adopted uncle, offered his family's farm as a venue. If it wasn't for Sophie's deep-seated horse phobia and Gemma's off-the-charts allergies, we would have jumped all over it. Instead, we're scouting locations with wait lists that stretch to the sun. As the early summer twilight sneaks in through our bedroom windows, I wonder if we'll still be searching for a place to get married this time next year. I just know Nick would have known the perfect place, and the known the right person to ask to secure it.

I scrub my hand over my face and turn to my fiancée, who chews the ends of her hair in deep thought.

"Are you getting close to shutting down?"

A non-committal hum is the only response.

"Jill?"

"Do you want carrot cake or angel food cake?" she asks, saving a slew of new cake designs as she cross-references it with our budget. Three of the cake vendors in town are so backlogged they aren't accepting orders for two full years out.

"At this rate," I say, "we'll have a Dairy Queen ice cream cake."

Frankly, it could be worse.

"I don't want ice cream cake. I want it to be perfect."

I shrug. "Relax, it's going to be perfect."

"It'll be perfect if I make it perfect," she snaps, and jerks her head up, shrinking away from me, and her voice comes out small and breathless. "Sorry! I'm sorry!"

The air in the room freezes. If I move a muscle before she does, all she'll see is an impending storm that she can't escape. That's not Jill talking. That's fear. That's self-preservation. That's years of her asshole ex-boyfriend exploding at her for expressing any emotion that wasn't quiet submissiveness.

And her reaction is at least partly my fault. "I'm sorry I dismissed your frustration," I say, quietly. "I don't want to tell you how to feel."

Years after leaving him, one false step, and the landmines he had set in her heart still detonate without warning. I will walk to the ends of the earth to clear them all, to help her heal, but it never should have happened. I honestly don't know what I'll do if I ever come face-to-face with that little prick.

For his sake, I hope I never find out.

She slumps against the headboard and hides her face behind her hand. "I'm sorry, too," she says, this time in her real voice. "I shouldn't have spoken to you like that."

Every time I show her she's safe with me, I like to think I help her heart heal. For now, I squeeze her hand. "What's going on?"

"It's just …" Jill fiddles with the edge of the bedspread. "I spoke to my mother today."

Ah. That's where the tension is coming from. The phone calls have been more regular since we told her parents we're getting married, and none of them have ended in tears or emergency therapy appointments.

"How'd that go?"

"My mother brought up paying for the wedding again." She shifts her face hiding behind the curtain of her hair. "I was telling her how hard it was to set a date because we couldn't get a venue, and she said she can use some of her contacts at the university to find something." She draws a breath. "But she'd want it in Toronto."

From the look in her eyes, she's seriously considering it. What surprises me, is that so am I.

It's not just the bakeries that are backlogged. Every venue on Jill's wish list is booked for two years.

I should know. I've called every one of them.

Unless we want to double our budget, we're not getting married until I'm forty. Either that, or we're pumping Sophie full of Valium and my sister full of antihistamines and having that country-themed wedding on Travis's farm after all. I'm still not sure I'd want my ninety-year-old grandmother bouncing around in Gemma's Subaru for three hours into the Rocky Mountain foothills.

And Toronto as a location? That's actually not a problem. Toronto would be a better destination for a lot of my relatives, being so close to Montreal. And leaning on her mother's contacts, whomever those might be? Lizanne probably has an in at some heritage building steeped in academic lore.

Be still, my nerdy, chemistry-loving heart.

But by the way Jill is humming, I'm not sure that's what she wants.

She's back to chewing on the ends of her hair. "What if this is a way she and I can heal our relationship? Have those mother-daughter moments that everyone talks about? Dress shopping, all that..." she trails off.

For me ... I don't know. I wouldn't put it past Lizanne to pull the *I'm paying for it* card to get what she wants. Jill has enough stories of her mother forcing her to have what she wanted without taking Jill's wishes into consideration. Her sweet sixteen was practically a debutante ball, despite Jill wanting to try horseback riding with her friends. Or her outfits being picked for family photos for years. Or having her bedroom painted the colour that her mother wanted (Buttercream) instead of what Jill had asked for (Violet Riot).

Did I paint our bedroom Violet Riot the weekend after Jill moved in? Take a guess.

Inviting her mother into our planning is a sign of hope over experience. A potentially futile one, at that, but not for me to decide. It makes sense, of a sort. Hell, we can get a bunch of the planning done when we are there at Christmas.

Which in itself will be a push. It'll be Jill's first Christmas home since her dickwad ex sprung a public proposal on her. First time back to Toronto since her mother spent months trying to convince her to work things out with him. Getting steamrolled with every decision, until Jill fled to the other side of the country for enough space to live her own life.

Maybe having me on Jill's side will be enough to prevent any steamrolling.

"If you think this is the way to work things out with you mom, and if that's what you want," I say, "then let's go for it."

She huffs out a breath, clearly relieved. "What do you want?" she asks suddenly.

For us to already be married and you not be so stressed that you develop ulcers. "For our wedding cake to be chocolate."

She snickers, and swats my shoulder. "Noted, but what else?"

I suppress a nervous chuckle, because I'm about to hedge the same way Jill just did moments ago.

"Now it's my turn to say I don't want to upset you, but—"

"No buts," she repeats. "Tell me."

"We didn't sit around braiding hair and plan our weddings in university," I say after a minute, "but I always thought Nick would be part of this. We went through so much together. He brought me takeout for a week when my girlfriend broke up with me and my parents divorced in grad school. He convinced me to pursue my PhD when everyone else said I should stick to getting my P. Eng. If I'd have stopped there, I'd be stuck behind a desk hating my life if I hadn't. Without getting my PhD, I never would have developed my tech—"

I stop as if my chest has taken a direct hit with a sledgehammer.

Without my PhD, we never would have started CMR. Campbell & Martin Remediation was his idea. If it wasn't for Nick, I wouldn't be in bed with my fiancée, planning our future together. "If it wasn't for him, I'd never have met you."

Jill squeezes her arms around my waist and shakes her head against my shoulder. "I would have found you."

"We would have found each other," I say gruffly. "Nick would have tried to convince me to have some stupid bachelor party that he'd back off from as soon as he'd ribbed me enough. Pushed for the groomsmen to wear 1970s powder blue tuxes. Threatened to add a bunch of ex-girlfriends to the invite list."

"Wait," she cuts in, a look of mock horror on her face. "You have ex-girlfriends?"

"No, Sweetness, it's only ever been you." I chuckle, then sober.

Nick saw the writing on the wall the day I spent my first free Sunday in months setting up Jill's office furniture instead of hiking, and she barely deigned to make eye contact with me back then. He gave me endless shit for that.

I shrug. "I miss the guy. The guy I used to know, anyway."

The Nick who had been *my* biggest cheerleader. Who did the schmoozing with the clients so I didn't have to. Who was full of stupid stories and good ideas.

But that was years ago. Time slips like water through my fingers, escaping no matter how tightly I try to hold onto it.

She's silent for a long minute, face pensive. "That Nick sounds like a good person," she says finally. "I'm sorry I never knew him."

"Yeah." I swallow a lump in my throat. "I wish you'd have known him, too."

5

TOWELS

Months engaged: *four*
Months to doctor's appointment: *four*
Months until wedding: *seventeen*

IT'S TAKING ALL MY WILLPOWER TO STICK TO ONLY TWENTY kilometres an hour over the speed limit.

The road trip to evaluate a site out west turned from three days into six. An old mining site had a whole host of issues that took way longer to determine if CMR tech exists to remediate it. The tech doesn't exist.

Yet.

But I've been working on developing this new strain of microalgae, and it's promising, and ... well, it doesn't matter. I was supposed to be home days ago.

"It's not like ... anything ... me." Her voice comes over the car's Bluetooth in choppy bursts. Even though I know it's the shoddy reception, it sounds like her voice is breaking, and guilt knifes me right in the gut. " ... not a big deal."

But it is a big deal. I promised her I would be home by now.

Instead, I'm stuck hundreds of kilometres away in a queue of cars speeding east through the Rockies. At least I don't need to worry about breaking down on the highway anymore. Gemma goaded me into replacing my car last year, and as much as it sucked retiring Anni-frid, it was the right move. If I would have known how much Jill stressed out while I was on the road. I'd have done it a year ago.

Did I get another Volvo wagon? Obviously. Had to order the yellow paint job special, but some things I won't compromise on.

Jill named this one Björn. For tradition.

This road trip going long is the most recent bump in a long list of challenges. I can't even be mad about it, because all the challenges have been good.

Jill's boss had her on track for a management position. Last week, we celebrated her promotion.

Ever since my student loans were paid off, we've been saving for a down payment on a house of our own and not renting from Gemma and Bea anymore.

After my last research results were published, a wave of new clients reached out with work, including the one that made me late coming home now.

Every single one of these are things we want. Things we dreamt of, planned for, wanted to achieve together.

And every single one of these have thrown a new complication into wedding planning.

Jill's promotion means longer hours and more responsibility, and when she's home, she's exhausted.

Gemma and Bea let us know they were planning to sell the house Jill and I live in. They are giving us almost a year's notice, but we won't have enough down payment to buy something by then.

CMR is thriving with the new business, so much so that I need to hire more help again. But hiring and training new staff takes time, and I'm stuck in another province for days instead of with Jill.

It's a huge pain in my ass.

And I'd promised her I wouldn't get stupid with work again.

"Bean, I—" I start, but the call drops as the road dips through a valley before she can respond. *Shit.* I toggle the Bluetooth off and twist the steering wheel like it's a throttle to supercharge the wagon faster, but I ease my foot off the gas a fraction.

Jill would kill me if I died speeding on my way home to her.

I bite back a chagrined chuckle and triple-shoulder check before I pull around a semi-truck slugging up the hill in front of me. Besides, the drive gives me time to think about the wedding planning we've done, or rather, how much we haven't.

No venue. No colours. No flowers or cake. Hell, we just got *Save the Date* cards sent out.

January 10: A week after my thirty-fifth birthday. I'm not dwelling on the fact that said date is eighteen months away. Deadlines usually kick proverbial asses into gear, but our asses remain unkicked.

The hours crawl by, with a construction delay as the cherry on top as I hit the city limits. I park Björn behind Jill's hatchback and shoulder my overnight bag. Wearing three days worth of clothes for a six-day trip in the late summer has left me rank. The only plus is that the clients I was visiting were farmers, and they couldn't care less if I came on site with a bit of stink on me.

A dull whir and guitar twang hit my ears when I open the front door.

My lip twitches. Is Jill listening to country music? *By choice*?

Claws scrabble across the linoleum and an eighty-pound tornado of slobber and hair barrels into me. I bend down to take the brunt of Daisy's affection to my chest instead of my knees, scrubbing the pooch's ears in rough circles as her tongue lolls out with happy bursts of panting. I give her a solid pat on her belly and go in search of my fiancée.

The whirring grows louder, the vacuum drowning out my footsteps as Jill's off-key singing reaches me from the living room, and I can finally make out what she's singing.

Beyoncé's country album. I should have known. It's been on repeat in our house for months.

Her back is to me as she pushes the vacuum around, with her free hand pumping in time to the music. I lean against the door frame to watch her dance with a dopey grin on my face, and wait for her to turn around.

I don't sneak up on her. I did, once, before we were living together. I'm a big man, and not quiet, but she had been so focussed on her book that she didn't hear me come up behind her to pull her into a hug. The unexpected touch sent her into a panic attack before I could calm her down.

When she could finally breathe again, she told me how Connor used to sneak up to scare her on purpose, claiming he was preparing her in case she was attacked if he wasn't there. All he managed to do was overdevelop her startle response into a near guarantee of a panic attack.

After two years of deconditioning, she doesn't jump when I touch her by surprise anymore, but I'm not chancing a backslide. She's had to deal with enough of those.

Two years, and I'm still undoing the damage that asswipe caused.

Fuck that guy.

Daisy shoots past my legs and butts into Jill's knees, and she turns around with a wide smile. She drops the vacuum with a clatter and launches herself at me.

Her arms wrap around my neck her and legs circle my waist. I scoop my hands under her ass to haul her against me. Our lips meet in a slow, deep kiss, our tongues tasting each other in a slow dance.

It's damn good to be home. Hugging my girl with our dog scooting around us, the summer sun streaming through the windows. I don't think I'll ever get used to this.

"I missed you, Cupcake," she says when we break apart.

"I missed you, too, Bean." I plant a kiss at her temple and bury my nose in her hair. Vanilla and honey, followed by a hit of the smell wafting off me, overpowering even her sweetness. Six days on a farm will do that, and I pull away with a grimace.

"Not yet," she muffles into my neck, tightening her arms around me.

If she can tolerate how I smell right now, I've fully Stockholm Syndrome'd her. I get it, though. I could huff her scent like an addict. So I do, taking in deep pulls of her sweet smell until she's squirming in my arms like a puppy. Still, this will be a lot more pleasant for her when I don't smell like old clothes and dirt.

"Let me take a shower," I say, and step out of her embrace to strip my shirt.

The corner of her lip sneaks between her teeth as her eyes roam over my chest. "Do you need any help?"

Let's fucking go. I sweep her into a bridal carry and march to the bathroom. "Just with the hard-to-reach spots."

By the time the water's warm, I've stripped her bare and reduced her to a giggly mess. She yelps when I slap her ass on the way into the shower. There's just enough room for us to maneuver. I position her under the water so she doesn't freeze, and get to work lathering myself up. Her hands are covered in suds, too, though as usual, she chooses to focus on my pecs, biceps, and glutes. Fine by me. I can take care of the less fun parts to clean.

I steal the soap back to scrub the last of the travel grit away as she continues to massage the soap into my chest. I duck under the stream to rinse, but when her touch grazes the V of muscle that points to my groin, the soap squirts out of my clenched fist.

Cleaning time is over.

My cock is at half-mast even before she wraps her fingers around my girth. After one hard stroke, it's at full salute.

"Fuck, Jill." My hips pump into her hand on reflex. The water is cascading over her, and she leans in to let her breasts brush against my chest.

My head lolls back as her hand slides to the base of my cock, her fingers roaming over my balls, and I suck in a breath as a jolt of desire zips down my spine. "You keep doing that, this is going to be a short shower."

"Don't worry about me," she says, sweetly. "I've been taking care of myself while you were away."

"Are you saying the showerhead replaced me after a few days away?" I growl.

"Well …"

She shrieks when I spin her around and place her hands flat on the tiles. Challenge accepted.

My cock is trapped between the small of her back and my stomach, and I have total access to her breasts and pussy. Her chest rises and falls in excitement as I run my hands over the flare of her hips, every inch of the smooth, slick skin I missed while I was on the road. I drag my thumbs over her nipples, her breath escaping in a soft hush.

"Your hands. So rough."

A week on the farm toughened the calluses on my hands. I tease her nipples into hardened peaks. "Want me to stop?"

"I was thinking," she gasps, arching her hips into me, "that I should send you away for hard labour more often."

"Then I'll just make sure you look forward to me coming home."

I part her thighs, my middle finger circling the tight bundle of nerves, before sliding a finger inside her. Her body tenses and relaxes at the same time, and a second finger joins the first.

Fuck, my girl feels so good, so tight around my fingers. She's going to feel fucking amazing when her pussy is squeezing my cock.

I let my fingers slide over her entrance, dipping in, pulling out, pumping into her, working her clit until she's on her tiptoes and whimpering my name.

Maybe she hasn't been taking good enough care of herself if she's already this close.

"Can your showerhead do this?" I ask, not breaking my rhythm.

A puff of air escapes her lips. "It—*ah*—it has multiple settings …"

Brat. Multiple settings, eh? I tap my finger, swirling and strumming, until her breath comes in jagged bursts. She's so close to her edge, grinding her ass against my hips, and I hiss out a breath. My cock aches for her, but I won't need to wait long. Seconds later she's bucking against me, feet slipping and knees buckling, as her orgasm snaps through her.

She's a limp mess, and I pull her upright, leaning down to drop a trail of light kisses on her neck. I catch a stream of water at her belly, scooping handfuls over her skin. Her head tips to the side, and she slides a shaky hand to cup my cheek behind her.

"Think you can stay standing?" I ask.

"Yes. No." She sags back against me. "Give me a second."

I'm already swiping my cock along the cleft of her ass. She's not getting another second. Six days is long enough. I can hold her upright.

I bend my knees until I'm lined up at her entrance, a soft moan drawn from her throat as I ease inside. The last traces of her orgasm flutter around me, and her wet heat grips me until stars form on the back of my eyelids.

Six days might as well be six weeks. I stop halfway inside to get control, but my body has a mind of its own, and I thrust deeper as she opens to me.

Fuck, it looks so good, seeing my cock get swallowed up by her perfect pussy. I give her butt cheek a light tap that sends a ripple across her skin.

"Jesus, I missed that ass."

"Is that all you missed?" Her laugh is cut off with the wet slap of my hips against her skin, and it sounds as good as it looks.

She's fully doubled over, gripping her ankles, trusting me to hold onto her, and I drive deep into her again and again, her ass jiggling with every thrust. Steam billows around us, hot water like rain, but all I feel is her.

"Alex—" *God,* I love it when she moans my name like that,

"—I'm so full of you. You feel so good, I missed you, please, harder ..."

My girl knows exactly what I want to hear, continuing in a steady stream of pleading that sets me on fire. She releases her grip on her ankles, pressing her palms flat against the tile to drive her hips back into me. A jolt rocks straight to my core. I'm so deep inside her, and I squeeze the soft flesh of her hips. I slide my fingers to work over her clit again, and her inner walls tighten around me as her orgasm builds again.

She's fucking me back as hard as I'm fucking her, our bodies slamming together faster, until her pussy clamps down on my cock and sends me over the edge.

"Fuck, Jill, *fuck*." A guttural cry rips from my throat as I come so hard the corners of my vision dim. My hips jerk once more as I drive into her, wave after wave of my release flooding into her.

It's almost worth going away to come home to this. That extra heat of missing her, breaking apart like a spell as we come together again.

I can't believe I get to do this for the rest of my life.

The water is still pounding on us. I stand in the spray so it doesn't get in her eyes, and pull her against me, stroking my hands over her back. She's wobbling on her feet, completely given up on trying to stand on her own. I'm weaving on my feet as it is, but I can keep us both up. And I'm not going to lie, getting her weak like this makes me proud as hell.

My cum looks so good dripping down her leg. The sight has me half-ready to go again. I kneel in front of her, swiping some onto my fingers and rubbing it over her clit.

"Do you have one more for me?" I ask.

"No. Please. Mercy," she gasps, squirming against me. "I'm so done."

I smirk, but relent. I'll get number three out of her later.

Instead, I rinse her clean, careful around her overly-sensitive parts, and even then my touch still makes her twitch.

"Can the showerhead make you fall over?" I ask.

She threads her fingers through my hair, pulling my face down to kiss me. Her lips are so soft against mine, and not at all helping the half-mast go away.

"Even if I fall, I know you'll catch me."

Every time.

A few more seconds of scrubbing for round two of cleaning, and I'm wrapping us in mismatched towels. Pink from her home, that she bought when she moved to Calgary. An threadbare navy bath towel that's travelled with me between who knows how many apartments.

It occurs to me that this is something that we could put on our wedding registry—the fluffiest new towels to wrap my future wife in, in whatever colour she wants—and my heart soars.

That day can't come fast enough.

"Can I show you a few ideas I had for the wedding registry?" she asks, tucking the edges of her towel in.

I laugh, cupping my hand around her cheek. "Funny you should say that."

6

MESSAGE (UNREAD)

Months engaged: *five*
Months to doctor's appointment: *three*
Months until wedding: *sixteen*

> GEMMA
> Jake forgot his socks yesterday
> I'll stop by after your game

THE SHARP BLAST OF THE WHISTLE CUTS THROUGH THE SUMMER afternoon, and the pitch clears as our teams file past each other to shake hands. My forearm is still bleeding from a rogue cleat, my kit is stained green from knees to shoulders, and the tape on my fingers is black with dirt.

Doesn't matter. We won.

I lift the hem of my jersey to mop my brow, and when I lower it, Jill is already bouncing to her feet and throwing her arms around me in a hug that smells like fresh cut grass and sunscreen.

"You looked so good out there!" Her mouth finds mine,

kissing me slow and deep, and I lean back to lift her feet off the ground.

I don't give a shit what the final score is. *This* makes me feel like I've won.

When I put her back down, my sweat brands her with a damp patch across her chest.

Good. Property of Alex. Remind everyone she belongs to me. Not like any of the guys on the other team are stupid enough to hit on her anymore.

It only happened once. During half time, at a game last summer. One of the guys on the other team was standing a little too close to her to be considered friendly. The expression on her face had morphed from indifferent to uncomfortable by the time I was jogging over to check on her.

Then he brushed a wisp of hair off her shoulder.

She had already given him a death glare and batted his hand away in the two seconds it took me to reach her. I ignored his wincing when I put him in a friendly headlock to steer him back towards his team, but I could've been more polite when I informed him that I would rip his arms off if he touched her again. Word spread quickly after that.

Just because my girl can take care of herself, doesn't mean she has to.

Jill laces her fingers behind my neck and tips her head back to look up at me. "Did you win?"

"What do you mean, did I win? You just said I looked good out there."

"I can only keep my eye on the ball or your legs." She shrugs with an impish grin. "I made my choice."

Brat. I click my tongue. "I'm just a piece of meat to you, aren't I?"

"Mm-hmm." she replies gleefully, and grabs my ass. "Alberta Prime beef."

If my future wife wants to objectify me, I won't complain. Instead, I bark out a laugh and tap her butt in payback as we head over to join my teammate, where Dan has already relieved his girlfriend of their squealing daughter. Half the guys on my team have families cheering on the sidelines now. Far cry from a few years ago, when most of us were single and would hit the bar for post-match bevvies.

Well, *they* would. Between finishing my dissertation and starting my company, I was so busy I only joined a couple of times a year.

Until Jill came into my life. She's always extolling the importance of grown-up playdates. Now I spend more time with my team than before I met her. Even today, I'd be stuck behind my computer if she hadn't dragged me here when she got home from volunteering.

Dan adjusts the sunhat slipping off his daughter's head. "Are you coming over with the crew?"

I rub a palm over the scruff on my chin. My playdate allotment for the week is up.

After coming back from the farm site last month, I got an idea. Which led to a side study. Which led to a new stream of research, which came back with unexpected—and promising—results.

The kind of results that could translate into a breakthrough in my process. Not to mention tens of millions of dollars in funding.

Actual *tens of millions of dollars*. That would keep the lights on at CMR for a long, long time. Cover a down payment on a house. Kids' college funds.

That only happens if I bust my ass to make sure my results are in order.

Which means between the lab, the office, and the field, I've put in almost a hundred hours this week. Carving out a couple hours for a game is a luxury I already can't afford.

"Ah, next time, Danny," I say, and Jill gives me a crooked smile. "Work's going to take me a few hours."

I know that look. She's not worried about getting enough

time with me. She loves solo time with friends. But it's not *her* work-life balance she's worried about right now.

"Just a few hours?" She twists a strand of hair around her finger.

When Jill and I first got together, I promised her I wouldn't get stupid about work again.

But here I am. Getting stupid.

"Maybe," I hedge. I blow out a breath and rake my fingers through my damp hair. It's more than a few hours, but Jill can go and have time with her people, even if I can't.

And if I bust my ass, I'll get through enough of my analysis that she and I can have dinner tonight. Maybe even have some time together tomorrow.

Time to bust some ass.

A car engine cuts, and Jill's car door slamming breaks my attention from the screens I've been staring at for who knows how long. Judging by the angle of the sun slanting through the windows, it's been hours.

Half a sandwich sits uneaten beside me. No wonder I'm starving. I lean forward, unsticking my skin from the back of my chair. I was in such a rush to start work I didn't bother to put on a shirt after my shower. I scrub my hands over my stubble. Right. Didn't bother to shave, either. Same story all week. Now my face feels like a hedgehog.

"Alex?" Flip-flops slap across the floor and keys clink onto the hook by the front door. The sun shines through the sheer sundress that swishes around her knees and the wisps of blonde hair sticking out from her messy bun. She looks like a fairy sprite, all lit up and airy.

Her brows draw together when she sees me at my desk. "You're still working."

The disappointment in her voice is a brick to my sternum. I'll do anything for this woman. Paint a bedroom purple. Buy her a house. Give her a perfect wedding. Whatever puts a smile on her face.

Except, apparently, stop working myself to death. Jill's given me the entire afternoon to focus on getting this done, and I'm not finished. I dig the heels of my hands into my eyes and hunch over the keyboard.

Her feet pad across the floor to me.

"Lean back."

Just knowing what's coming has tension releasing from my body.

Her hands smooth over my piano-wire tight muscles. First gently, then harder, each stroke of her hand along the cords of my neck working out another hour of stress I've piled onto myself. Her elbows dig into the knots on my shoulders, leaning her weight in.

I tip my head back against her breastbone as she works her fingers in circles over my temples, and after several minutes, ninety percent of my stress has evaporated.

Call me putty and wrap me around her finger. No one in the world gives a neck massage like her.

"What are you working on?" Her voice is soft and clear, the ends of her hair tickling my forehead as she leans over me.

"New contract came in at the same time as a critical testing phase."

"Are you done?"

I grunt.

A soft hum vibrates through her chest. "No breaks?"

Another grunt.

"Oh, Alex."

I sigh. "I just got caught up again."

Her thumbs dig into my traps, and my shoulders loosen further. "Do you need to focus, or do you need a distraction?"

There's something in her voice that makes me interested in learning what distraction she has in mind.

A look of complete innocence greets me when I peel my eyelids open.

"Distraction?" I tug at the end of her sundress until she's standing in front of me, her dress ruching in layers as I slide my hand up the inside of her thigh. I hook my thumb on the waistband of her panties. One tug and they hit the floor, and goosebumps prickle under my hands as I brush my fingers over the curve of her bare ass. "What kind of distraction do you have in mind?"

"I attended a webinar on wellbeing." She throws a leg over my thighs to straddle me. "They said if you've been working on a mental task for a while, you should do something physical to shift focus."

"Physical?"

"It sounded well-researched," she confirms. "Very scientific."

"You're pulling out the 'it's scientific' argument?"

Her hand slides into my shorts. "I'll pull out whatever it takes."

Consider my focus shifted.

The straps of her sundress slip down her arms. Her skin radiates the day's heat, lightly sunkissed and flushed from the heat. I swipe my nose along the column of her neck and peel her top down. Sweat beads along her collarbones, and I lick my way to her breasts. She's salty, and warm. She's summer wrapped in a sundress. Her nipples harden under my tongue, and she arches into me with a muffled sigh.

She sucks my fingers into her mouth before guiding them to her pussy, and I let out a hiss as I work my fingers over her clit.

"Yes, Alex, like that." Her lips whisper over the rasp of my stubble, breath warming my mouth. She sucks my bottom lip into her mouth, and she tastes like lemonade. "I need you inside me. Stretch me. Fill me, please."

Jesus, my cock is going to rip through my shorts. It makes me feral when she whispers my name, telling me what she wants, with her breath gentle on my lips, like I can swallow her words and make them a part of me.

My index finger dips into her heat, then middle. I want to add another, do what she wants. Stretch her until she moans, but I've got something else that will fill her up properly.

The quiver under my hand grows stronger as I thumb her sensitive bundle of nerves until she falls against me, her nipples hard against my chest. The little whimpers that escape her as she comes have me grinning into her hair like a goddamn fool.

I kiss the fluttering pulse at her throat, slowly withdrawing my soaked fingers. "Are you ready for me now?"

"Wait," she pants, her pussy still clenching my fingers. "Do want me on my knees instead?"

"I want you exactly how you are."

Right now, I need to be inside her.

I shove my shorts out of the way. She lifts up on her toes to fit my cock at her entrance, holding my gaze as she lowers, aching slow down my length. Time stretches as she takes every inch of me, pausing to catch her breath, until her ass hits my thighs.

"Oh, fuck." I clamp my hands over her hips to stop her from moving, but I can't stop her inner walls gripping me like a vice. The peaks of her nipples dance within mouth distance, begging me to take one between my teeth.

"You keep moving like that," I grit out, "this is going to get really embarrassing for me."

She squirms, trying to roll her hips. "I don't want to keep you away from work for too long."

I'm so done. I lean forward to catch a nipple in my mouth to tease her with my tongue. She rolls forward into me again, picking up speed, and the chair gives an ominous creak.

If we're not careful, we're going to break another chair.

She bounces on my cock like I'm her personal fucking trampoline. My balls tighten as she increases her pace, holding her open even as she tips over the edge, clamping down on me as she comes apart. I lose myself in her shaking around me and grip her hips to work her up and down, my arms burning with effort, until I spill inside her. Pulse after pulse, I jerk into her one last time, and drop my head against her shoulder.

We're just a rush of breath, a tangle of limbs. She collapses against me, fingertips lazily stroking the hair at the nape of my nape. I pull back far enough to kiss her. Her eyes are unfocussed, body pliant. She nips at my bottom lip, looking completely satisfied.

Stretched and filled, just like she asked. And she got me to stop working.

My girl always gets what she wants.

"Good distraction," I say, and she giggles, but a noise at the front of the house makes any post-coital endorphins evaporate.

Our heads swivel as the front door crashes open, and two pairs of feet thunder the short distance from the front door to the dining room table where my office is set up.

Where my fiancée is still sitting astride me, naked from the waist up.

No time. There's just no time. I yank her top up and cover the rest of her nakedness with the skirt of her dress. I wrap my arms around her in a bear hug to keep the top from falling back down and seal my lips together.

Whether I'm suppressing a howl of laughter or a barrage of curses, I'm not sure yet.

"Uncle Sandy, what are you doing?" Jake asks as he comes to a stop in front of me.

I am so unprepared for this.

Don't make a big deal. Everything is cool. They don't know what's going on.

"Having grown-up time, bud. Can you go wait for your moms outside for a few minutes?"

"S'okay, they're coming."

Just perfect.

Jill is shaking in my arms. "Oh my god. This is happening,"

she manages to cough out. I'm not sure if she's laughing or crying. Probably both.

My innocent, clueless nephew rocks on his feet. "Are you working?"

"Remember when you were asking about a cousin?" I say, and Jill's shaking increases. "We're working on that."

"Yeah! Hen! We're gonna have a cousin!" Jake whoops, attempting a jump spin.

Henry trots up beside his brother and narrows his eyes at my open laptop. "Do they come from Amazon?"

Serves me right for encouraging them to ask questions.

"Where are your moms?" I ask in a strangled voice. "Can you go tell them to come back later?"

"Mama!" Jake twists his body to scream in the direction of the open door. "Uncle Sandy and Auntie Jilly are having grown up time and want us to come back later!"

I groan. "Not what I meant, bud."

"What?" my sister calls out. Seconds later, I hear footsteps over the kitchen linoleum and then her shrieking, "Jesus, Alex! What the hell?"

So much for being cool.

"I think it's time to teach the boys to knock before going into someone's house," I say, doing everything I can not to burst out laughing. "Can you get your kids out of here?"

"Honey, don't come in here!" Gemma bellows to her wife, trying to herd her sons out while avoiding looking in our direction. She half-turns to me, a hand dramatically shielding her eyes. "I texted you we were coming over!"

"I obviously didn't see it," I grumble.

Jill is no help. She hasn't budged, arms still wrapped around me and face hiding in my neck, a light vibration running over her body. I adjust the covering of her skirt. "Give us five minutes?"

The front door slams, and silence rings through the empty kitchen, leaving Jill and I alone at the dining room table. She's rigid with laughter, arms crossed over her chest to hold her top up as tears run down her flaming cheeks.

She hiccoughs, wiping her eyes. "We've scarred them for life. We're going to need to set up a therapy fund."

"Nah, I covered you in time," I assure her. "The boys didn't see anything."

It couldn't have been twenty seconds from door opening to them leaving. Half of the guys on my team have a mortifying story of one of their kids accidentally walking in during, ah, grown-up time.

I slide the thin straps of her sundress over her arms and kiss where it settles over the hollow of her collarbone.

"Gemma and Bea are never going to forgive us," she says, feathering her lips over mine.

"My sister has forgiven me for worse things."

Like when I punched out a homophobe for calling her some choice names. Or the time I stole one of her teen magazines, trying to figure out why my stomach felt funny when I looked at the girls in the pictures.

My hands settle on Jill's waist, and I ease her off. We've made a beautiful mess. I'm dripping out of her, smeared across her thighs.

I want to fuck it all back inside her now. But that's not happening.

Two inquisitive boys with the worst timing will bust in here again any second. If they can stand to look at us, Gem and Bea will probably stay for dinner. Not to mention wedding details we've been meaning to talk to them about.

I'm definitely not getting any more work done today.

I couldn't be happier.

7
NAME

Months engaged: *eight*
Days to doctor's appointment: *three*
Months until wedding: *thirteen*

"You're sure you don't mind?"

"I'm sure."

"You won't be uncomfortable?"

"I'll be fine, and you'll be uncomfortable if you don't."

"It costs more." Jill chews her lip, fiddling with the dial.

"It's your house, too," I remind her. "Turn up the heat as warm as you want."

We had this conversation last year, too. I didn't figure it out until I noticed her lips were blue. Her ex kept their shared apartment at roughly the temperature of a cave, and wouldn't let her change it. She was still too nervous to change it on her own.

Jill twists the dial of the thermostat one last click. The old furnace gives a dull thump, followed by a whoosh of warm air, and she gives a relieved sigh.

Old habits are hard to break. The first time she set the thermostat where she wanted, she cried. My therapist says loving a person after they have been mistreated takes patience, communication, and understanding. If Jill wants to make it tropical inside while the first cold snap of the year rages, we can afford to shell out a few extra dollars to give her a sense of control. Anything to keep her happy.

And if it means she'll keep walking around wearing nothing more than my old U of C hoodie, crew socks, and pink cotton panties that show a lot of cheek? That keeps me happy.

Jill shuffles over to where I'm lying down on the couch and throws herself prostrate between my thighs. "Did you hear Cass and Libby are filming outside tomorrow morning? I bet they are filming the chase scene."

Our friends are nearing the end of shooting the film adaptation of one of Jill's favourite books. When I told her they were using my lab for a scene, she nearly left work to come watch, but Josh, the intense and surly director, demanded a closed set, with no nonessential people permitted. I was given a pass, since it was my lab they were using, and I needed to be on site to make sure they followed safety guidelines.

Realistically, though, standing around, waiting for shots to get set up, waiting for Libby to reposition lights, waiting for Cass to fix the lead actor's costume? It wasn't that interesting.

What *was* interesting was finding out the grumpy director couldn't keep his eyes off Cass. She wasn't much better. I was halfway tempted to keep them away from any reactive compounds in case they sparked a fire. Maybe it was good they'll be in a farmer's field, fully clothed in subzero temperatures tomorrow.

"Bet they'll find a way to stay warm," I say.

Jill giggles, kicking her feet up behind her and resting her chest against my crotch as she scrolls through itineraries for her visit to Montreal next week.

Wedding planning is progressing. Slowly. We have colours (lilac and navy) and flowers (peonies and something called baby's breath). A fancy-ass place Jill's mother was angling for in Toronto had an opening ... four months after our wedding date.

Lizanne said we'd be fools not to make a simple date change to secure the venue. Four months' delay wasn't too much to ask for, especially after all the hard work she'd done to secure it for us.

We declined.

The hockey game on TV barely holds my attention. Maybe if my team wasn't getting their asses handed to them I'd be able to focus on something other than the curve of Jill's ass in my line of sight.

All the websites say not to have unprotected sex a week before getting an IUD removed to prevent pregnancy, but since that's literally the goal, who knows why we are following that rule.

Oh, wait. It's because I'm getting married to a woman who considers rule following an Olympic sport.

I love that she follows the rules, even ones I hate. Like this one. It's actually cute, and *usually* there's a good reason for it. Not like I'm saying that out loud right now. And it's not like we aren't having fun in other ways.

But even when she was on her knees yesterday, nails scraping my thighs and tongue swirling on my cock, it isn't the same as being inside her.

For the record, this is not a complaint.

But now it's been four days and having her wedged between my legs with her face hovering over my stomach isn't helping.

Four days down. Three days to go. I can wait three days. I refocus on the game and try to ignore my fiancée's boobs pressing against my junk.

"I'm still not sure."

"About a dress?" I ask, thinking about the stores she's planning on visiting with Sophie.

"About the name."

I huff a breath out my nose. One hand is tucked behind my head while the other hand winds a lock of Jill's silky hair around my ring finger. The ends tickle my chest as I let it spring free. "You've got time to decide."

"I just hated growing up with a hyphenated last name," she continues, waving her socked feet back and forth like windshield wipers. "I dropped Saigner as soon as I got to university. I don't want to do that to our kids. And it's not like there's any pressure to either keep it or change it anymore. Everyone just does what they want. Pilar took Kyle's name. Gem and Bea kept their last names."

I wind another strand of her hair around my finger. *Sproing*, it pops free. If she keeps rubbing against me like this, her hair won't be the only thing *sproinging*.

Whatever she wants, whatever she's most comfortable with, I'll be behind her no matter what.

It's just a name. That's what I keep telling myself.

"I can legally change it but keep my maiden name for work," she muses. "I can be Ms. Northrop in the boardroom, and Mrs. Campbell at the PTA meetings."

My inner caveman perks up. *Wife. Mine. With my name*. Blood flow redirects straight to my dick, and I shift so she doesn't notice. "Yeah," I jump to agree. "Mrs. Campbell sounds really good."

She gives me a soft smile and drops a kiss on my bare torso. Damn, this woman is killing me tonight. I fix my stare at the tv and ignore the sparks she's sending through my body, wishing her butt was in grabbing distance. At least I get to look at it from here.

"I know I'm not the first woman to grapple with this. I just feel like I'd have to turn in my feminist card."

"It's not unfeminist if you want to do it," I say absently, still taking in the view.

Jill drops her phone on my stomach. "Did you just ..."

What did I *just*? My finger stalls in fiddling with her hair.

That's her *I've out-maneuvered you* expression. The one she gets when she's figured something out about five seconds before I have.

And then it hits me. "No, I didn't."

"You're mansplaining feminism to me!"

"No," I repeat, horrified. I already don't like what's coming next. I snatch her phone from my stomach before she can grab it and hold it out of reach. "You are not texting Gemma."

"Gimme!"

I wrap her close enough she can't make another break for her phone and rat me out to my sister. Not like that matters. She's still trying to squirm out of my grasp like she's navigating a Tough Mudder event.

"Promise you won't tell her."

"I—" she gives one last attempt to break free before she tires and slumps against me, breathless, "—promise."

I don't believe her for a second.

This is my favourite: feeling her melt against me. Body soft and warm, any tension worked out and all that's left is a relaxed puddle of Jill. Wrestling is just an excuse to get her into this position.

Gemma used to say that she wished I'd have been a girl so she could have had a sister instead of a stinky brother. Now, she jokes that I made it up to her by bringing home Jill. If I'm honest, I like how they gang up on me. And if Jill wants to narc me out to Gem, I can take whatever chewing out coming my way.

Jill gives me a sweet smile, then snatches her phone from my hand. She taps out a quick message and seconds later, my phone pings from the other side of the room.

Honestly. Gemma doesn't let me get away with anything. Neither does Jill.

In fairness, I did just mansplain feminism to her.

Jill drops her phone on the coffee table and grins at me. "I'll take it that you're putting in a vote for Mrs. Campbell."

Yes. "If that's what you want."

"Is it unfeminist for me to say I kind of like this little traditional streak of yours?" she teases. "Next thing you'll want me barefoot and pregnant in the kitchen."

The image pushes every other thought out of my mind. Jill in short-shorts and a tight tee shirt, all glowy and round with my baby inside her. Tucked up at the kitchen island as I cook for her to sate some weird pregnancy craving she's having. Just watch it be something like pickles and cilantro ice cream.

My heart feels like it's going to push through my sternum, I want it so bad.

It also has no reason to sound as hot as it does, and I shift to hide my cock twitching in my sweatpants.

Her soft smile turns playful, and she wiggles against me. "It sounds like you really like that idea."

I grind my teeth together and exhale forcefully through my nostrils. "If you keep doing that," I grit out, "I will drag you into the kitchen right now."

She presses her breasts into me, and blinks at me with those wide grey eyes of hers. "And then what?"

Her yelp fills the room as I bolt up, tossing her over my shoulder and stomping across the house into the kitchen. Her fists rain down on my back like drum beats, her breathy giggles abruptly stopping as I shrug her off, her butt smacking onto the kitchen island. The play-fighting isn't over yet. She aims a couple more half-hearted kicks at my torso, grinning like mad, but I trap her ankles around my waist and hold them with one hand behind my back.

My mouth finds hers, and I lick the seam of her lips open until she's panting against me. I pull her socks off, one at a time, and drop them on the floor.

"Barefoot in the kitchen. Now we're halfway there," I say. "I'll get you pregnant in here next week."

"Want to practice?" Her eyes are mischievous as she tightens her legs around my waist and returns my kiss, soft and slow, her fingernails drawing lazy designs on my scalp. A delicious shiver crawls up my body and another pillar in my will to resist her puffs into smoke.

Yeah, she knows how to play me.

She lifts her arms overhead to let me strip my borrowed hoodie from her. I kiss my way down her throat and over her collarbone. Each nipple gets attention, swirling my tongue, her whimpers buried in my hair as I suck.

I'm going to make a meal of her.

I slip a finger under the band of her underwear, and she nods at me with glassy eyes. I pull the cotton down her legs and add it to the pile of her clothes on the floor.

The swipe of my tongue along her centre is a spark, and her thighs fall open for me. I love how she spreads herself wide, head thrown back, giving me total access. I slick my fingers along the outside of her pussy, sliding a finger through her wetness. She shifts her hips as close as she can to the edge without falling off the counter. I draw her clit between my lips and sink a finger inside her.

God, she's so warm and tight. I trace my tongue over every sensitive fold, taking my time tasting her until she's shivering with need. If I didn't need both hands, I'd fist my throbbing cock to get some relief. Instead, I press her thigh open wider, driving my tongue deeper in time with the sounds that she makes.

"Don't stop, yes, right there, *please*," she begs, the last words a barely coherent plea.

Anything she wants.

I lap at her clit, coaxing my finger along her G spot until she's rocking into my face and digging her heels into my back. I don't know what her other hand is doing, but one grips my hair, pulling me away even as she moans for me until her legs are shaking. Her walls shudder around my fingers as a final cry rips from her throat.

She sags back, and I want to crawl up on top of her and fuck her right here on top of the kitchen island.

But rules.

I pull back, leaving a last kiss on her stomach and a wet smear behind as evidence. My beard is soaked. I rough the back of my forearm to clean it, then lick her juices from her belly. She tastes like dessert. Her hip bones jut out less than they used to, now that I have her eating enough. I can't wait to see the flat plain of her stomach swell with our child.

Soon.

She slowly raises her head, cheeks flushed and lips parted, her chest heaving as she tries to catch her breath. She peppers me with kisses, and I see a desperate look in her eyes.

"Alex, I want you inside me."

I swear under my breath, face pressed into her chest as I fist my erection through my sweatpants. It's all I want right now. To be inside her. Close to her. Physical touch is how we connect, and the more parts we have connected, the better.

But the doctor said no sex for a week. And if she's wavering now, I have to be the responsible one.

I hate it.

"Three more days, Jillybean, then I promise I will bend you over this counter and get you pregnant right here before dinner."

"I can't wait that long." She's nibbling the spot on my neck that makes my eyes roll back in my head, and she shoves my hand away from my dick so she can take over. Her fingers close around my base, and my balls tighten in anticipation. My hands have a mind of their own, wandering over every one of her curves, and she hums in approval. "I need you. Please."

Fuck. This woman is going to kill me. I know I'm supposed to be the strong one, but the words aren't coming out. I shift my hips into the tight circle of her hand, urgency building, struggling to remember why I'm resisting her.

Right. Three days. I can wait three days, but I can't ignore her teasing licks along my jaw. "The appointment—"

"What if you pull out," she whispers in my hair, fingers trailing over my bicep, "then we can take a shower together after."

Once I told her she was a terrifying negotiator. Like I said, she gets whatever she wants.

My sweatpants are around my ankles before the words are fully out of her mouth.

I tug her butt off the island and bend her over, already swiping my cock through her centre. She's still shivering as I ease my way inside, and I fold my body over hers with a low groan.

Take my shirt. Take my name. I'll give this woman everything.

"Fuck, I love that pussy," I whisper against the back of her neck. "Is that better?"

A soft whine escapes her throat, and she rocks into me in response.

I'm a smart man. I can take a hint.

I wrap an arm under her hips and proceed to test the structural integrity of our kitchen island. Every one of my thrusts push her farther away from me, and I yank her closer.

"More," she begs. Her legs are shaking, hands splayed out for leverage. I drive into her faster, deeper, her round ass slapping against my hips. I reach my hand between her thighs to stroke her clit, and her walls tighten around me.

The shiver coursing through my body alerts me approximately one second before I need to pull out. I bite down on her shoulder as I come in my fist. Hot spurts leak between my fingers and drip onto her bare ass, our skin sticking together as I spill onto her. I shudder, arms and legs tingling, gasping something incoherent into Jill's ear as I struggle to stay standing.

"I love you, too," she's saying, and I realize she's repeating my words.

I take a final deep inhalation and huff it onto her neck with a chuckle. I want to fold her into my arms, but my cum is running out of my hands.

Fuck it. We're taking a shower now, anyway.

I pull her back into my chest, nuzzling her neck until she's squirming against me. "In three days," I growl, "I'm not wasting another drop."

Heat flashes behind her eyes. "I'll take everything you give me, Dr. Campbell."

Anything you want, Mrs. Campbell.

8

IN SICKNESS

Months engaged: *eight*
Days to doctor's appointment: *zero*
Months until wedding: *thirteen*

Today has been literally and metaphorically circled in gold sparkly pen on the kitchen calendar since the moment Jill suggested that we start trying for a family.

A growler of amber ale is chilling in the fridge. Dinner prep is complete. Her favourite album is playing on the Bluetooth. I even booked her a hot stone massage after her doctor's appointment this afternoon, to relax.

Booking a massage after getting her IUD yanked seemed the least I could do. The work I get to do for conception is easy.

Put me in, Coach. Glad to be part of the team.

Headlights dance on the backsides of the curtains and tires crunch through the snow on the driveway.

She's home.

A surge of adrenaline dumps into my system. I drop the dish towel on the counter and pace, shaking out my arms.

Holy shit. Holy shit. Holy actual shit.

Here we go.

It could take months. A year or more. It might not happen at all. Or we could get pregnant right away.

I glance at the fresh bouquet of flowers on the dining room table as Daisy races past me to the front door. The keys jingle in the lock, and the tell-tale sound of stamping feet knocking snow off boots travels down the short hall from the front door to the kitchen.

"Who?" her muffled voice sounds confused. "Have I met them?"

My jaw clenches before she even comes into view, the tension rolling off her words in waves. She looks …

Anxious.

And my heart drops.

Tense posture. Tight voice. Sharp movements. Her body language is quietly screaming.

I don't need to ask who's on the other end of the call.

The furrow between her eyebrows shrinks and expands as she listens. She holds up a finger in the universal *just a second* signal, and slouches into the living room to dump her bag, giving Daisy an absent-minded scritch under her chin. I follow her into the living room and squeeze her shoulder.

"Okay, sure." One hand grips the phone to her ear, and the arm wrapped around her stomach slides up to cover my hand with her own, her fingers turning white as they grip mine. Her shoulders sag. "Yep. Love you, too."

When she disconnects, she tosses the phone on the couch and drags me to the bedroom.

"Weighted blanket."

Oh, shit. It's that bad.

Weighted blanket is code for *I've had a terrible day and I don't want to talk about it yet but I need you to squish all the stress out of my body with yours.*

It's surprisingly effective.

She flops on our bed, fully clothed, and drags me on top of her. A deep groan pushes out of her lungs as I lower my weight onto her, propping up on my elbows so I don't suffocate her. She wraps her arms around my back and hides her face in my neck. Daisy, having followed behind us, looks at me for permission. At my nod, she jumps into bed and curls up at Jill's feet.

There's a part of me that wants to reach inside her brain, find everything that has ever upset her, and extract every last bit of it to shoulder it myself. Make it so she doesn't have to grapple with the anxiety that flares up.

If only I could. I know I can't. All I can do is bet there for her. And occasionally act as her personal human weighted blanket.

Put me in, Coach. Glad to be part of the team.

Her heart rate is already slowing, a steady thump against mine. Good. No panic attack on the horizon. I stroke the hair back from her temple and plant a kiss there.

"Hi, Bean."

"Mmfph."

"Is that code for 'I can't breathe and I need you to get off me?'"

Her arms tighten around me. "Not yet."

Time to break out the big guns. This calls for the extra heavy weighted blanket.

Slowly, I ease off my elbows and drop a few more pounds of weight on her, and a few more, and a few more, until I've created a Jill-sized dent in the mattress.

A laboured *eerk* squeaks from under me and she pushes at me with a tired grin and a gasp for air. I roll off, pulling her with me, cradling her in the crook of my arm with her cheek pressed to my heart. We lie there in the dark, with the music fading into our room from down the hallway as her breathing slows, inhaling and exhaling in time with me.

Jill burrows into my side like she's trying to crawl under my skin. "Hi, Cupcake."

I respond with a nuzzle.

"The flowers are really pretty," she whispers. "Thank you."

Peonies. Her favourite. The florist even had them in lilac.

After a few more minutes of comfortable silence, she says, "That didn't hurt nearly as much as going in, but the doctor's version of light cramping is a lot different than mine."

I swallow a pang of guilt, like it's my fault she had to get one in the first place. That fault lies with her shithole ex, who tampered with her birth control on more than one occasion. Getting the IUD was the only way she felt safe. She would have had to take it out eventually, even just to replace it, but I still hate that she's in pain. And that there's nothing I can do.

"I'm sorry you're hurting." I don't just mean physically.

She shrugs. "Then my period came while I was on the massage table, and I bled through the sheets. I was so relaxed I didn't realize it until I got off the table. It was so embarrassing. And my mother called on the way home, and she wants to have an engagement party when we are there, and invite all these people she works with. And then I felt selfish because I didn't think you'd want a party, but my mother said you'd want to meet them because you're in their field, so I agreed."

I groan inwardly. Crowds of people I don't know is the opposite of my idea of a good time. But with my research in the phase that it is, I can practically hear Nick's voice screaming in my ear to rub elbows with these people. Three years ago a networking opportunity would be the exact sort of thing he would have taken off my shoulders. Now, it's all on me.

"Thanks for thinking of me," I say instead.

She takes a shaky breath. "And she wants me to wear her wedding dress."

I draw back to meet her gaze. "What?"

"She said it could be my 'something borrowed.'" She tucks her head back into my neck. "She's insisting."

There are two reasons Jill is heading to Montreal next week. The first is to tear up the city with Sophie and Kyle for Sophie's birthday. The second is to shop for wedding dresses.

There's a whole other Pinterest board I'm not allowed to look at that she and Sophie have been adding to for months. I haven't seen a photo of her parents' wedding, but my guess is that whatever Lizanne wore thirty-five years ago looks nothing like what Jill wants today. Judging by her face, I'm sure of it.

And I already see her folding to what her mother wants, trying to keep the tentative peace.

But if it means Jill isn't going to be happy, then that's not the kind of peace I want to build. I take a deep breath, and keep my voice quiet. "No."

"But it could be a new tradition …" she trails off.

Her mother's fingerprints are all over that idea. One more way her mother is trying to exert control. I'm tempted to tell Lizanne if she wants everything in her vision, she should have her own wedding.

"You are going to wear what will make you feel beautiful and special on your day, not what someone else dictates. Not for a tradition that doesn't exist, or one you don't want to start."

The last of the tension drains away. She knew it. She just needed to hear it.

"I'm so tired of fighting her." Her voice hitches, and her fingers curl into a fist around my tee shirt. "And tonight was supposed to be so special and you planned so much and I'm really sorry I ruined our night."

I sigh. Here I am, focussed on railing my future wife, while she's had a piece of metal yanked out of her vagina, dealt with a period blowout, and fended off an overbearing mother. No wonder she's had a shit day.

And she's still worried about disappointing me.

Tonight's going to go a little differently than I thought. No problem. We have a whole lifetime of romantic evenings ahead of us.

"You didn't ruin our night," I say, extracting myself from under her. "Why don't you take a nap while I cook dinner. I'll wake you when it's ready."

"You're not mad?" she whispers.

"Never."

That's a lie. I'm livid. But not with her.

What infuriates me is that she spent a lifetime being treated so badly that she expects people who claim to love her to get mad when things don't go according to plan.

She's already looking at me with sleepy eyes, her smile watery at the edges. "You take such good care of me."

I'm trying my best. I'll try every damn day for the rest of my life.

And as long as she knows that—feels it in her bones—that's all that matters.

9

AND IN HEALTH

Months engaged: *eight*
Months until wedding: *thirteen*

She's been in Montreal for a week, and I've done everything I can to keep myself busy until she gets home. A week of hitting the gym and the trails and the lab. A week of going to bed alone and waking up on her side of the bed with my face in her pillow.

I don't know who moped more: me or Daisy.

A cheerful *ping* bounces off the lab's sterile white walls, and I scramble for my phone.

> I just landed 🩶
>
> Are you at the lab? I'll meet you there

The last time we had sex was two weeks ago. As soon as she got her IUD yanked, she got her period. Then she was on a plane for Sophie's birthday.

I have been counting down the seconds to this moment since the day she said she wanted to start our family. My self-control is waning.

If she comes to my lab, I'm fucking her beside the Bunsen burners.

Jesus, keep your dick in your pants until you're home. I count to ten, and type a reply.

> I'll be home soon. Promise.

Already on my way 😊

Like I'm going to be able to focus on my work *now*.

My latest experiment has been culturing for months, and the good thing about microalgae is that it won't care if I ignore it for a few more minutes.

Jill launches herself at me as soon as she is through the lab doors a half an hour later. Even from the short trip from the cab to the lab, ice crystals frost the tips of her hair, the tip of her nose bright red peeking out from under her fleece scarf. Her lips are cold on mine, but her smile is bright as moonlight on a winter night. I grab a handful of her butt as I haul her against me, and she wraps her legs around my waist.

"Hi, Cupcake." Her voice muffles against my shoulder. I run my nose along her neck and my heart squeezes behind my sternum.

I missed this. All of this. My Sweetness. My Jillybean. Her smile and smell and how tight she holds me, no matter how long we've been apart.

She unwinds her legs from my waist and kisses me, and I remember I am the luckiest man in the world.

A lucky man who *absolutely can wait* until he gets home to impregnate his woman.

The same set up as two weeks ago waits for us at home. Flowers, dinner. Hell, the bed has fresh sheets, so I'm ready to pin her on her back with her legs in the air for an hour to get this to take root.

Will we pull out all the stops every time until we conceive? Probably not, but the first time should be special.

A dull ache squeezes my balls, and I step back and cross my arms so I don't rip her clothes off right here.

I lean against the table and cross one scuffed Blundstone over the other. "How was the weekend? Leave out no detail."

I told her not to worry about checking in while she was away. Connor had put enough limits on what she could do. She's a grown woman, and she's had enough of someone keeping tabs on her for this lifetime.

She still sent me good morning and good night texts everyday, and about a hundred photos of holiday lights, between snaps of her and her two best friends ripping up the city like they used to in university.

The glow in her smile as she details her week makes the time apart worthwhile.

"I'm glad you had fun, and even more glad you're home," I say when she finishes her tales.

Jill shimmies forward on the bench, with a sweet-as-sugar look. "How glad?" she asks, and sneaks her fingers around the button of my jeans.

The desire I've been tamping down sparks to life, and I flick a glance to make sure the lab's security door is firmly closed. "Here?"

"Why not?" she asks. Her hand is already cupping my thickening cock through my boxers.

This might be biased, but labs are a dark horse, sexy-ass place to fuck. Sure, they're bright, but that means you can see *everything*. Cold, but that makes sliding into her warmth that much more intense. Private and secure, so she can make all the noise she wants and not worry about anyone stumbling in on us.

And clean. So I can fuck her on any surface I want.

But romance. Dinner. Making love in our bed with mood lighting and post-coital snacks as we start our family.

I resist one last time. "Are you serious right now?"

Without another word, she pulls my cock out of my pants, drops to her knees, and licks a long stripe up my shaft.

Jill knows how to win a debate.

My eyes shutter closed when she sucks my crown into her mouth. She's taking me so agonizingly slow, her lips wet and warm. When she can't take me any deeper, she hums when I hit the back of her throat.

She draws out her retreat, swirling her tongue as she releases my cock from her mouth with a wet *pop*. Her thumb smooths through the bead of cum on my slit while she drags her tongue over my balls like I'm a fucking ice cream cone.

"Hot Jesus fuck," I groan out, and bite down on another gasp. "Hot Jesus fuck."

"You've mentioned that. Anything else you have to say?" she asks, and slides her mouth down my length again.

Can't. No words. Lust floods my torso and shuts down my synapses. My entire world is this stunning woman looking up at me through dark lashes, swallowing my cock like she hasn't eaten in a month.

For once, I don't want to come in her mouth. Before I get too close, I pull her to her feet and roughly kiss her, stripping her pants off as I plant her ass on the table.

"Spread."

I lick the crease of her thigh, and mouth her pussy over her cotton underwear. The fabric is dark with her wetness already. I want to eat her, for her thighs to clamp down on the side of my face and block out all sound until all I hear is her muffled moans. I tug the damp material aside to suck one of her lips into my mouth. She's sweet and tart and dripping for me. I release her from my mouth and blow lightly over her clit.

"No showerheads in Montreal?" I ask, and breathy laugh erupts from her throat as she rocks her hips into my face.

Her orgasm crests like a tidal wave. Under the bright light of my lab, she's the most beautiful thing I've seen in my life. She grips the back of my head, her back arched, and I suck her clit into my mouth as she lets out a strangled cry.

The soundproof walls of my lab are coming in handy.

When her shaking stops, I kiss my way up her body, over her shirt. We were in such a rush we didn't bother undressing.

"God, I missed you."

"Then show me how much."

She's still shivering from her orgasm as I swipe my cock through her folds. Her pussy is dripping, she's so ready for me, and I don't think I've ever been this hard in my life.

I pause, one hand around the nape of her neck, the other at the base of my cock, ready to guide myself into her. My heart is beating like a bass drum against my ribs.

"We're really doing this," I say.

"We're really doing this." She takes my face between her hands and kisses me. "Put a baby in me."

Fuck.

Get inside her.

Now.

Primal urgency takes over. I bury myself to the hilt in one stroke. It's wild, and raw. I slam into her over and over.

"You feel"—I wrap a hand under her ass to pull her closer—"perfect."

A sharp gasp drags me to my senses. I can't tell if it came from me or her. I drop my forehead against her neck, my shoulders bunching up as I curve my body around her. Our mouths find each other, tongues tasting, and she sucks in a breath as I hit her even deeper.

"Alex, *please* …"

"What do you want? I want to hear it."

"You."

Hearing her say my name, *begging* me, drives me harder. "You can take it," I growl. "Take it all."

My muscles ache from the effort of driving into her. I brace against the tabletop, folding her backwards. She's so close. She's mine. Her legs are bound around me, her nails digging into my shoulders. And when the head of my cock hits deep in her core, she trembles around me again.

Her thighs and pussy clamp down on me, gripping me everywhere, as her orgasm shatters through her. Her cries wordless against my mouth unleash the last of my restraint. The pressure building around my spine snaps, and I let out the harsh roar in my lungs.

And I fill her, and fill her, and fill her.

It doesn't end. Waves pulse over me and flood into her. Every ounce of energy and cum and love pour out of me, and she takes everything I give her. I collapse forward onto the table as I gasp through the last shudders.

My senses trickle back. I'm wrapped in Jill's arms. The lab's AC on my bare ass. The bite of the metal table on the front of my thighs, where I have Jill trapped under me, her breathy laugh in my ears. I blink hard, shaking my head to clear the last of the fog.

"Holy shit," I gasp.

"Alex…"

"That was …"

"Alex…"

"Incredible."

"I can't breathe."

I pull back, laughing as I unpin her from my lab table. My other half. My future everything. But I don't have the words, just the feeling that being with her makes me feel complete in a way I never knew I needed.

I hiss in a breath and pull myself from her. Cold air hits our sweat-damp skin, and a cascade of goosebumps prickles Jill's skin. My cum leaks out of her, painting a streak down the crease of her thigh. I give in to my urge, and swipe it up with my fingers to shove it back inside her.

It wasn't supposed to be like this. I pluck tissues from the dispenser and clean her up, dropping a kiss on the little mole right beside her belly button.

"So much for staying on my back with my knees against my chest."

"I had this whole plan. There's flowers and candles at home," I say a little sheepishly. "I was going to make you tacos for dinner."

"Alex, this was perfect." She kisses me. "And you can still make me tacos for dinner."

"It's a deal." I stand back to zip my jeans back up with a chuckle, and catch her as she tries to stand. She sways on her feet, and I push her to sit beside a collection of slides beside my new microscope, waiting for my attention.

The slides will have to wait. This is officially now a task for Future Alex. I have no interest in being stuck here any longer.

Who knows how long it will take us. Nature isn't on a schedule. But if we conceive today, I'm telling our future kid we made them in a lab.

The door clicks open behind me as Jill slips back in as I finish clearing my work station. Her skin is still flushed and eyes sparkling, and my heart melts. She steps into my outstretched arms again and rests her cheek on my chest.

"Can I take you home?" I ask.

"You had me at tacos," she says as I lock the door behind us. She looks up at me with a cheeky grin. "I was thinking that if we get pregnant in here, we can tell our future kid we made them in your lab."

10

MESSAGE (READ)

Months engaged: *nine*
Months until wedding: *twelve*

> **GEMMA**
>
> I have something for Jill, but don't tell her yet
>
> I'll stop by later
>
> FOR THE LOVE OF GOD TELL ME YOU GOT THIS MESSAGE
>
> > ffs that was one time, Gem

"What do you think?"

The ivory ribbon sits coiled in a rough wooden box. A few threads fray out from the worn edges, a few smudges on one end, but it shines under the lights of my office.

My throat swells, and I swallow the wave of emotion. "I think Jill is going to cry her eyes out."

"Probably," Gemma says. "I did, when Bea's aunt gave it to me."

I can't pretend I remember seeing the ribbon wound through Gemma's bouquet when she got married. Flower arrangements weren't exactly on my radar back then. Besides, I was too busy dodging one of Bea's cousins from hitting on me all night.

It feels like a lifetime ago.

Four generations of women have had this ribbon incorporated into their wedding attire. Veils, hems, bouquets. Now my sister is offering an heirloom from *her* new family to welcome Jill into *ours*.

My ribs cave around my heart, and I pull my big sister in for a hug.

"Thanks, Gem," I choke out.

Yeah, my girl's definitely crying.

"I'll offer it to her when you get back after Christmas. No pressure." She stashes the box in her satchel, and gives me an encouraging smile. "Are you ready to meet her parents?"

I blow out a breath. "I'm nervous as hell," I admit.

She wallops me on the shoulder, grinning. "It'll be fine. It's her family. They love her. They'll love you. How bad can it be?"

11

ROOM

Months engaged: *nine*
Months until wedding: *twelve*

THE SLUSH IS UP TO MY ANKLES WHEN I STEP OUT OF THE CAB. ONLY a few degrees below freezing, but the damp crawls under the collar of my jacket and leaves icy fingerprints on my neck.

Grey bricks, grey planters, grey snow. The entire scene looks like someone desaturated a photograph.

I give a double-take at the size of the house. From everything Jill's told me, her dad did well as a private sector financial advisor, but unless the University of Toronto has a wildly different pay scale than the U of C, her mother must have some wild speaking deals under her belt. Professors usually make enough to put groceries on the table and a decent car in the driveway, but not the driveway of a large detached home in a well-heeled suburb. At least, not in today's market.

Got to love good old Boomer timing.

I flex my hand to get the blood flow going again after Jill releases it, and hoist our suitcases out of the trunk. She trudges past the patches of dead grass peeking out from the snowy lawn, up the shovelled walkway to the front door. I shoulder our bags and follow, her hands shoved in her pockets to pull her jacket tight across her chest. She raises her hand to knock, and pauses with her knuckles inches from the door.

"I grew up here. Why am I knocking?" she mutters under her breath, not moving.

Because it doesn't feel like your home anymore. I wonder when the last time it did. I put the suitcases down and wrap my arms around her. She's so stiff, it's like hugging a statue.

"We can still get a hotel," I offer.

To stay with her folks, or not. The discussion went in circles for weeks.

Pros: Lizanne, Arthur and I will have lots of time to get to know each other. Plenty of room. Great location. Not footing the bill for a week in a hotel in the most expensive city in the country during the Christmas season.

Cons: her parents.

Her mother, really. I don't think I need to list the reasons why.

Jill shakes her head. "No hotels. I've got this," she says, and blows out a breath. "No. I don't. I feel like I'm going to barf."

No wonder she's nervous. It's the first time she's seen her parents in almost three years.

Three years of no contact, then low contact. Three years of finding herself and finding her voice. Finding a way to trust her instincts again.

Now thrown into her childhood home for a week, armed only with a hundred hours of weekly therapy sessions and the olive branch of letting her mother into wedding planning.

Jill rolls her shoulders, tilting her head from side to side. "Focus, Northrop." She lowers her hand from the door and turns to me. "Am I still going to say 'Focus, Northrop,' when we get married, or will I start saying, 'Focus, Campbell?'"

My heart jumps. She hasn't said what she's decided yet. Maybe she's getting close. "You're deflecting," I say, hedging, "but 'Focus, Campbell' always worked for me."

She gives me a narrow-eyed look, but she's smiling again, and her shoulders aren't wound around her ears anymore.

Four crisp raps, and I follow her inside.

"Jillian?" A voice I recognize from a few phone calls and numerous panel talks floats from another room and echoes across the entry way's vaulted ceiling.

Jill rolls her eyes. "What a stupid power play. She would have been watching for us from the window. She could have been downstairs ready for us."

Even after watching the family dynamics via phone for two years, I get the feeling that I'm underprepared for the real life experience.

A series of increasingly loud clicks is followed by Dr. Lizanne Saigner's showy entrance, arms and smile stretched wide, her husband trailing steps behind. "Oh, dear, it's so *wonderful* to finally see you again!"

Jill lets herself be pulled into a stilted hug, air kisses dusting her cheeks. "It's good to see you, too."

"Careful. This creases," her mother says, passing Jill over to her husband and running her hands down her blouse. She turns to me. "Alex. What a pleasure to finally meet you in person."

I don't know if her smile is always so bright and cold, but it looks like she's analyzing her next move. My dad taught me at age fourteen that men as big as us don't approach women quickly. I keep my feet where they are and extend my hand. "We actually met when you gave a talk at Yale back in—"

"Oh, shoo," she says, waving my hand away and stepping in for the same feathery embrace Jill received, who's still crushed in her dad's bear hug. "I met a fresh-faced new graduate student that day. Not that I remember you. I met so many people that day!" She titters, and tilts her head in a move that is eerily similar to Jill's when she's thinking.

But where her mother is all sharp and cold, Jill is all softness and sunshine. Her mother flashes that bright smile again. "Now I'm meeting my daughter's boyfriend."

"Fiancé," Jill corrects as her father releases her, and her mother titters again.

"Silly me, my mistake."

Mistake. Sure.

Her mother releases me and I shake Jill's dad's hand, exchanging pleasantries and confirmation that yes, traffic sure is terrible this time of year and indeed the wet cold of Toronto is different from Calgary's dry cold.

If we're not careful, we'll cover how bad the Leafs are doing this year and run out of small talk before dinner.

I'm not the smoothest at meeting new people—Nick was always the charming one—but I'll do the best I can. Whatever it takes to get Jill through the week.

"Well," Lizanne claps her hands together and turns to the hallway, "I'll show you to your rooms."

Jill pauses on the first stair, her hand already on the bannister. "My room is upstairs, unless you moved it?"

"Of course you'll be in your room," Lizanne replies, "and Alex will be in the guest room downstairs."

Five minutes in the door and we already have our first hiccough. Jill blinks at her mother. "You know we live together, right? Where we sleep in the same bed?"

"But you two aren't married yet, and we've never let boys stay in your room before."

Boys? I'm less irritated at being classed as a *boy* than Lizanne insinuating she had to limit a parade of sleepovers her daughter tried to sneak in.

"When I was a child. I'm an adult now."

"It's only for a few days." Her mother *tsks* with a shake of her head. "I don't see why you need to turn every little thing into a production, Jillian. You're getting everything else you want."

Ah, so this is how we're being punished for not going with her mother's wedding dress. I wondered if that was going to bite us in the ass.

Jill nods slowly. "It's only for a few days. I understand. Your house, your rules," she confirms, and my heart sinks until she follows it up with, "We'll find a hotel close by."

I swell with pride. A few years ago, my girl would have puked before standing up to her mother. Now her voice is steady, even if there is a flush creeping up her neck. She reaches behind her back, and I take her hand to interlace her trembling fingers between my own.

"Jillian." Lizanne smiles like a shark. All teeth and no warmth. "Don't you think that's a bit dramatic?"

"Nope. I think you're being perfectly reasonable. You've explained your boundaries, and what you need to make you comfortable. I respect that. Now I will explain what will make me comfortable. I am not going to be separated from my fiancé when we don't have to be, so we'll find other accommodations."

This sounds like a rehearsed speech. All of a sudden I know what the last-minute session with her therapist was all about.

It's a standoff. Neither Jill nor Lizanne budge. I'm opening my mouth—to say what, I don't know—when Arthur steps forward with a nervous laugh.

"Jillian and Alex can take whichever room they prefer. The downstairs guest room might even be better," he says, looking tense. He closes his eyes and continues, "It has more privacy."

I imagine he's not wanting to think of his little girl all grown up. Or maybe it's speaking against his wife, who's smile remains rigidly in place. Either option can't be comfortable for him.

"Of course." Lizanne says, eyes trained on her husband, who's avoiding looking at anyone.

"I appreciate that, Arthur." I hoist our luggage and follow him down the long hallway. A seating area off to our left shows a gallery wall of family photos, and my eyes land on it immediately.

The photo of Jill and Connor at a friend's wedding from the summer before she broke up with him.

Jill hates that photo. Hated walking by it every day. A reminder of how he controlled her. It's too far away for me to make out the details, but after being with her for over two years, I recognize the tenseness in her posture even from this distance. She begged them to take it down, but for some reason, her parents keep it up.

It's such a small thing to do. If someone I loved asked me to do some small thing to make them happy, I would do it without hesitation.

My fingers itch to remove it, but it's not my house. I don't want to make any waves.

We've been here five minutes, and already I'm counting down until I can get her home.

"Before you get settled in," Lizanne says, "There's been a change of plans."

From past her father, I see Jill's shoulders ratchet up a millimetre. "Oh?"

"The original venue for the engagement party isn't available. I tried so hard to find something else, but nothing was available on such short notice. Deborah has graciously extended her home for us to use instead."

"Deborah's house," Jill repeats, and freezes with her hand on the guest room doorknob.

"Yes, Jillian. I didn't realize I had spoken so unclearly that you couldn't understand me the first time."

"No, I heard you." Jill drops her head into her hands and presses her fingers into her temples.

Deborah. Lizanne's best friend. Connor's mother.

The last time Jill was in that house, Connor had sprung a proposal on her in front of a hundred people. Jill had made her escape from him that night.

I glance at her, trying to gauge how I can support her. I shift the luggage in my grip. "What's wrong with the original venue," I ask to buy time.

"Oh, don't worry about the details."

"That's awfully convenient," Jill says. "The one place I wouldn't want to go is the one place available to us?"

"You are always so suspicious," her mother laughs. "Their house is so much better set up to host than ours. You spent half your high school years there. It was practically your second home."

A second home that turned into a prison, but I don't think saying that out loud will help Jill right now. I try to catch her eye over her father's head, but her eyes are screwed shut.

A stilted silence fills the hallway, until Jill finally gives a resigned nod. "And you promise Connor won't be there."

"He's not even in town."

The tension ebbs from Jill's posture. "Out of town?" The relief in her voice is palpable. "Okay."

There's no deceit on Lizanne's features. Just the same brittle expression she was wearing when we arrived.

There's also a niggling itch in the back of my brain I can't scratch.

"So," Arthur says, coughing awkwardly. "How about them Leafs?"

Dinner conversation is going to be a treat.

Almost exactly two years ago, Jill paced the bedroom in my grandmother's house, vibrating with nervous excitement minutes before meeting my family. Less than an hour in this house and anxiety rolls off her in palpable waves as we get ready to have dinner with hers.

The shower washed away travel grime, but did little to ease her nerves.

Our suitcases are laid open on the queen-size bed. Mine is a jumble of bunched up tee shirts and jeans. I scrub my hand over my jaw and adjust the towel around my waist, debating whether or not it's worth the hassle to unpack for the week we're here. Jill is already marching between the bed and her overpacked suitcase, half-dressed, her towel already drying on the heated warmers in the en suite.

It nearly exploded open when she unzipped it, but she's packed so much to be prepared for anything her mother throws at her. From the scheduled family dinner with an aunt and uncle she barely knows to the engagement party where we were instructed to *dress to impress*, who knows who we'll be impressing. I just hope the singular suit that I own is impressive enough.

Jill scurries by again, another load of clothes from her suitcase dumped into the drawers of the gleaming oak dresser, her hands wringing as she goes to dive back into the bag. A path is already worn through the vacuum lines on the carpet where she's been treading back and forth. Meticulously rolled or not, by stuffing the suitcase as tightly as she did, her clothes will have as many wrinkles as mine.

Saying that out loud will not be helpful right now.

Instead, I snag her out of her pacing to pull her into my lap. Tension rolls off her, so thick I can almost taste it. Being in the same room with her mother is like adding too much reactant to the wrong solution, bitter and volatile. I wrap my arms around her waist until her breathing slows, deepens, and releases in a long sigh.

"I'm really proud of you," I say.

"Thanks." She swallows, grimacing. "I feel like I'm going to barf."

No surprise. Standing up to her mother is her number one trigger for an anxiety attack. But she did it.

"I think now I know why you like breaking rules," I murmur against the shell of her ear.

Jill hums a question against me.

"They've all been stupid."

The laugh she stifles turns into a snort, and the last of her tension evaporates. After a long minute, she says, "She's going to make my dad suffer for that. If you weren't here, she'd give us both the silent treatment. With you here? Who knows."

If it means Arthur having to deal with the fallout, I almost feel guilty for not sleeping in separate rooms. Almost.

"I can't take responsibility for her actions, only my responses," she recites the script her therapist taught her. "There would have been a time I thought that was my fault, but now I know it's just how she works."

The little game back there was likely not even about us sharing a room. Her mother just wants control.

I tighten my arms around her, and say nothing.

"Do you think it was a mistake to let her help with the wedding?" Jill asks for the millionth time.

That's the question I avoid every time she asks. I don't want to lie to her. Right now, I'm not about to tell her I think that her mother is going to find a way to throw a wrench in things. That old patterns will assert themselves, and Jill will find herself sucked into a vortex of passive aggressive negativity. Not when she just did an incredible job standing up to her mother for the first time in person. Probably for the first time in her life.

"I think," I start carefully, "that you give your mother a lot of grace."

"Sophie would say too much."

"Sophie is right."

I feel Jill's smile against my neck. "Did you pack your suit?"

"Mm-hmm." I nod to the garment bag already hanging over the closet door. All I need to do before the *dress to impress* night is iron it.

There's going to be a crowd of people I don't know, and a few people in my field who I would have given a kidney for five minutes of conversation with at any conference. The guest list isn't secret, but neither Jill nor I have seen a full copy. I get the sense that Lizanne has been trickle-truthing Jill with the final details.

I brush my lips over her ear. "You're doing so well."

"It doesn't feel like it," she whispers.

If she is stressed now, getting into actual decision making with her mother is going to be a grind.

"One week until the party. Nine days until we go home," I say.

She fiddles with the edge of my towel. "That sounds so long."

The tuck around my waist loosens. Her hand slides into the opening and tickles the sensitive skin on my stomach, and my body shakes off the fatigue of a day of travel.

"Bean … " My voice grows husky as her fingers scratch light circles through the trail of hair below my belly button, and my cock thickens in response. I glance at the bedroom door. Locked. My dick doesn't seem to care that her parents are down the hallway, or that I'm trying to make a good impression.

Last time I checked, good impressions don't include defiling daughters in their childhood homes.

Still, I can't help the smile forming on my lips. "What are you doing?"

"Since technically we aren't in my room, we wouldn't be breaking any rules."

I don't need to ask if she's serious.

The bed lets out a quiet groan under us as she turns to straddle me, plucking at the towel wrapped around my waist. One more tug and it falls open. A gravelly hum escapes my throat as she wraps her fingers around me and gives me a slow squeeze.

Every touch dumps oxytocin straight into my bloodstream. I stretch into her grip, sliding my hand up her thigh.

So much for making a good impression on her parents, but if my girl needs to release some tension, I'm here for it. I know my priorities.

"Fuck," I groan, and catch her lip between my teeth. Her mouth is warm and minty and opens to mine with a sigh. I work my hands under her shirt, over soft skin and flat tummy, to palm her breasts, swiping my thumbs over her nipples. A puff of breath escapes her lips as I brush each sensitive peak, back and forth, as she rocks along my erection.

Squuuuuueak.

We freeze, but the bed frame bounces another metallic twang off the blue walls. I lock eyes with Jill. The whites show all around her grey irises, and she slaps a hand over her laugh.

"Shit," she hisses between her fingers, pressing her lips together to hold back another giggle.

I feel like a teenager, sneaking into my girlfriend's room, trying to get some under the shirt action before they catch us … which is exactly what we're doing.

Except now I'm a grown ass man whose fiancée wants to get a little naughty before we're called to dinner.

My ribs creak with repressed laughter, and when I shift to regain my balance, the bed lets out another exaggerated screech under us.

"Do you think they rigged it to do that?" I strangle out. There is no way we are doing anything other than breathing in this bed without it sounding like we are testing out a rusty trampoline.

Jill shushes me, and tugs me to my feet. "Floor."

That's my girl.

Jill is many things. A quitter isn't one of them.

The bed releases a final groan when we roll to the ground. It's all I can do to not burst out laughing. Jill is stripping her shirt, and my hands are on her before it's fully off.

I drop to my knees, licking the swell of her breasts. "Tell me what you want."

With a cheeky grin, she reaches behind her back to undo her bra. "Your mouth."

This woman gets what she wants.

The cotton triangles fall to the floor, and I suck a perfect nipple between my teeth. A flick of my tongue sends a shiver flashing across her skin. Her fingers claw into my hair, and I tug her underwear down until they tangle at her feet.

God, she feels *lush*. She's so warm, so soft. Like her body is ready for me already.

She whimpers as my fingers leave her breasts and slide down her body to her ass. Damn, she has a fine ass. I knead her hips, knowing I'm going to be gripping her here to pull myself deeper into her in minutes. I swipe my middle finger through her heat, parting her folds.

"So wet for me already."

"When I said I wanted your mouth," she whispers, "I didn't mean to use your words."

I pull back, narrowing my eyes at her. It's a good thing she's cute.

"You are a brat," I warn. What I wouldn't do to give her a healthy tap on the ass, but the sound would likely magically magnify like every other noise in this room.

I trail kisses down her belly, through the light triangle of hair between her thighs, and breathe in her scent. I want to push her back onto the bed, hold her thighs open until she's splayed out before me so I can feast. The only thing stopping me from pushing her back is the protests the traitorous bed would make. Before I can suck her clit between my lips, she pushes a hand to my sternum.

"On your back, Dr. Campbell. I want to ride you."

How did I get this lucky? If she didn't already have me on my knees, I'd drop to them in front of her now.

In a brief bout of clarity, I toss a towel onto the floor. Carpet burn is a small price to pay, but I'd rather not explain any cleaning fees to her father.

I'm flat on my back, ready to pull her on top of me, when she turns around to face my feet as she straddles my face.

Oh, let's fucking *go*.

Her ass takes up my entire vision, her pussy hovering a tantalizing centimetre from my face. I wrap my hands around the backs of her thighs to pull her to my mouth.

Heaven. She tastes like heaven. Wet from the shower, wet from thinking about me. She quivers when I lick the edges of her entrance, like the anticipation is too much. Before I can spread her with my tongue, she engulfs my cock in warmth.

My brain fritzes as she swirls her tongue around my crown, and the answering hunger for her flashes along every limb. "*Fuuuuuuck.*"

"Still using your words."

Message received.

My tongue dives deep. A long, satisfied moan pulls from her throat, humming against my tip. Her pleasure washes over me and I pull her more firmly against my mouth.

She's rocking into my face, my cock buried deep in her throat. I spread her lips and circle my tongue around her clit, and the cascade of her orgasm flows right into me. I don't give her a second of rest. I flip her onto her stomach and slide into her with one slow thrust until I'm buried in her as deep as I can go.

"Not going to last," I gasp. I'm already so close from having her take me so deep in her throat. My hips jerk once, twice, and she takes everything I give her while she shakes to pieces under me.

I muffled my last groans against her neck. White imprints where I'm gripping her hamstring slowly return to her normal creamy pink, and I roll to my side in a boneless heap, pulling her with me until I'm cocooned around her.

The cool of the room would usually prickle her skin with goosebumps, but even with her shower-damp hair, she radiates a steady heat. She shimmies her hips to tuck against my groin, and cozy and nestled into me. Even on the floor, as long as I'm with her, I could stay like this for hours.

Or at least until we have to go for dinner.

"I'm so happy you're here with me," she whispers.

My heart squeezes in my chest, and I grip her chin, turning her mouth to meet mine. Her swollen lips. Her taste. Her scent.

Every soft fold and slick inch of skin. Every anxiety attack and nightmare. All of her. I wouldn't have her any other way. Just exactly as she is.

"No matter what happens, I'll always be here with you."

12

CONNOR

Months engaged: *nine*
Months until wedding: *twelve*

THE NEXT WEEK IS A TRIAL.

Nothing but walking on eggshells and dodging half-veiled barbs. Dinners with strangers and awkward conversations. Christmas morning is an uncanny show of white decorations and white clothing and white wrapping paper. White everything. I feel like I've been snowblinded.

Lizanne eyed Jill's red sweater and my green one as we unwrapped presents, like we dare break the aesthetic with colour. But her mother said nothing. She didn't need to. Enough was said in silence.

Wedding details are the only thing that keep me sane. Not the menu planning or seating arrangements or centerpieces. Just knowing that at the end, I'll be her husband.

Husband.

Eyes on the prize.

But first we need to get through this engagement party.

The SUV's front doors slam in quick succession, leaving Jill and I alone in the back seat. Lizanne is already clipping up to the front door, her designer trench coat billowing around her, with Arthur a few steps behind.

A hundred people wait for us inside. I'm sweating through my undershirt already, and my tie feels stuck under my Adam's apple. Still, my nerves are nothing compared to Jill's.

She spins her engagement ring around her finger, the small sapphire catching a stray beam from the streetlights. Her shoulders are wound around her ears, like a spring ready to snap under tension. The lipstick she carefully applied before we left is already chewed off in the short car ride over.

"Are you ready?" she asks.

A low chuckle slips out of me, and I cover her hand with mine. "I was going to ask you the same thing."

"There's going to be a lot of people here tonight," she says. A guilty edge creeps into her voice. She loosens the knot in my tie and pops open the top button of my shirt, and I suck in a full breath. "I know this isn't your idea of a good time."

"Any time with you is perfect," I say. I get out and cross to her side to open her door. She puts her small hand in mine as I help her out of the vehicle. "We've got this."

Light spills out of the house's picture windows and across the lawns. The walk stretches before us like a gangplank over shark-infested waters. Waters that appear to have been sowed with lots and lots of money.

Coordinated holiday decor weighs down every surface from the potted firs lining the walkway to the balcony railings to the front door. Music pipes through hidden speakers, flowing into the sound from inside, where her mother and father are waiting for us with the hosts.

Jill hadn't been kidding. This family goes all out.

Classical music and the artificial scent of evergreen hits us when we step into the foyer. A look of grim determination is etched across her brow, mouth set in a pasted on smile.

Nervous, but in control. No panic attack on the horizon.

The last time she was here, Connor sprung a proposal on her

in front of everyone. If my hunch is right, most of those same people are in attendance this evening. As long as he isn't, we can get through tonight.

It feels like we're playing with fire.

Jackets are lifted from our shoulders and air kisses are brushed above cheeks. Before I know what's happening, Lizanne has her arm linked through mine and is pulling me across the room.

"I have so many people to introduce you to." Lizanne reels off half a dozen names as she steers me into a gaggle of people I recognize from trade magazines.

I toss a glance over my shoulder, where Jill's father is pulling her into a conversation on the other side of the room. Our eyes meet, and she gives a helpless shrug.

"Won't they want to meet Jill?" I ask.

"Unless we get you alone for a few minutes, we'll never get a word in edgewise! You know how she always hogs the spotlight."

"I don't, actually." That's not the Jill I know, but the barb feels like a trap I don't recognize. "It's her wedding. Isn't she supposed to be in the spotlight?" I ask, instead.

Lizanne waves a hand as if to bat away my question.

At the event that is supposed to be celebrating our togetherness, I would have thought we would be greeting people as a couple. Never having been to a formal engagement party before, maybe this is how they are done.

I hate it.

"Dr. Campbell!" A woman with steel grey hair and wire-rimmed glasses beams at me, her bony hands clasped around my own. "What a pleasure to meet you! I taught your research to my grad students for the last two years."

I can only nod, stunned. Her work on mycological enzyme resistance was foundational in my first stream of research. I feel like I'm shaking hands with Dolly Parton. And she's using *my* work.

Just as I find myself agreeing to give a virtual lecture to her students in the new year, Lizanne steers me to a new group. I can't decide if I feel like I'm being put through a gauntlet or a welcoming committee. Half the people size me up like they are withholding judgement. The other half gush about my research and want to collaborate.

Jill wasn't kidding when she said I'd want to meet these people.

Every few minutes, I lift my head to search the crowd for Jill. Off with her father, a plastic smile pasted on her face.

She's holding up. A knot loosens in my stomach, but I don't let her out of my sight for long.

Meanwhile, Lizanne passes me from person to person. I feel like more of a show dog than a future son-in-law. I half-expect her to pull back my lips to show off the excellent quality of my teeth or ask me to display my haunches.

Something sits uneasy at the back of my skull. An itch I can't scratch. I shake more hands while I try to figure out what that is. I've received more congratulations than I can count, but the itch keeps itching.

Until something changes in the air.

Half my attention snaps from the monologue someone is spouting at me. I scan the room, and my blood runs cold when I find her.

The whites show around her eyes, skin pale. Her fingers bite into her elbows, shoulders caving inwards. Her entire posture radiates distress. And she's not alone.

I knew I shouldn't have let us get separated tonight.

He stands with an affected casualness, one hand in a pocket and the other clutching an empty highball glass. It takes a second look to see his flat stare and clenched jaw as he looms over her.

I'm already crossing the room without excusing myself from the conversation, leaving a confused voice at my back. My steps eat up the distance between us, and a second later, I wrap my arm around her waist.

A wave of relief flows from her as she melts into me. "Alex."

"Hi, Sweetness." I brush my hand over her bare arm, and take in the man who is glaring at me with such poison I feel like I need to chug a double-dose of anti-venom.

There's no sense pretending I don't know who he is. I don't want to cause a scene, so I tip my head as politely as I can manage. "Connor."

There's also no sense trying to shake his hand. He wouldn't return it.

And I wouldn't be able to stop myself from crushing his fingers.

A few guys flank him, shifting from foot to foot and glancing around the room. They must feel the same danger I do. One of them plucks at Connor's suit jacket's sleeve, trying to steal back his attention, which Connor shakes off with an irritated scowl.

For every emotion I thought I would feel in this moment—rage, vengeance, murder—it never occurred to me I'd feel calm.

As long as I stand between Jill and him, this piece of shit isn't worth my anger.

Barely contained aggression simmers under the surface of his glare. It's hard to tell if he's drunk or high, or if this is how he always is. He's an inch or two shorter than me, but he tilts his head back in an attempt to look down his nose at me.

"So," he says. "You're the boyfriend."

No scene. "Alex. Her fiancé," I correct, and his mouth twists.

"You weren't supposed to be here." Jill's skin is a delicate shade of green, and she swallows thickly. "You were supposed to be out of town."

"I was, until I heard you were coming home." He flicks a dismissive look at me. "You and I have years of history. You owe me a conversation."

The emphasis on *history* makes the canapés curdle in my

stomach. I force my hand to remain relaxed at Jill's waist, and ball my other hand into a fist in my pocket.

"She doesn't owe you anything."

"I wasn't fucking talking to you," he spits at me.

"Maybe not," I reply, "but Jill's made it clear she has nothing to say to you."

"Not even to say she's sorry? For bringing *you* here?"

"I was invited," I say. "And she has nothing to apologize for."

Connor scoffs.

Jill's pallor hasn't lifted, and she shrinks into me further. All the networking and rubbing elbows in the world isn't worth this amount of stress on her. If her parents or anyone has an issue with us leaving early, they can deal with me. "Jill, say the word, and we'll go"

A conversation beside us breaks off, and I can feel the stares cut through the chamber music still playing. I scan his friends. No one makes eye contact, either with Connor or me. I can't tell if they are chickenshits or embarrassed by his swagger.

"Come on, C-man," one of the friends says with forced bravado. "Let's get out of here. We have better things to do."

"No, this is what I want to do," Connor says loudly. He sets his empty glass on a side table with bang, and a few more people glance our way.

"Alex." Jill's voice isn't much more than a whisper. "I don't want to be here anymore."

Neither do I. If what Connor says is true, and someone—and I can guess who that is—slipped it to him that Jill would be back in town, then there is no reason to stay.

It might be throwing fuel on the fire, but fuck him. My woman needs me. I kiss her temple, not breaking eye contact with the fuming man in front of me. "Let's go."

"Are you that much of a beta?" Connor sneers. "You do whatever she says?"

Great. No surprise he turned into a red-pilled, alpha-male

wanna-be. Like taking care of your partner is a weak thing to do. I keep my voice level. "Yes."

"Fucking wimp," he mutters.

Diffusing situations was always Nick's forte, not mine. I grind my molars together. "Look, man. Just walk away."

"I'm not going anywhere in my own fucking house."

A few more guests peek in our direction, and Jill cowers into my side.

This isn't getting any better. I turn to one of Connor's friends. "You might want to get your boy to chill out."

"Please," Jill begs, her voice fading. "Leave me alone."

"I forgot how much you talk," Connor says, rolling his eyes. He turns to me with a conspiratorial smirk. "Just curious, the only way I could get her to shut up was to stick my dick in her mouth. Does that still work?"

A thick crack reaches my ears before the pain in my hand registers, and Connor's head snaps back as he buckles to the floor with a dull thump.

It'd be a lie to say I'm not angry. I'm more furious than I've ever been in my life. From the moment Jill told me how this waste of space treated her, I've ached to give him what he deserves.

It was long overdue, and satisfying as fuck.

"I told you to walk away."

Honestly, I'm glad he didn't.

"You son of a bitch," Connor slurs, grasping at his friends' shirts to struggle to a stand. "Pathetic cuck."

This fucker is begging for it. I flex my aching hand and will it to stay at my side. "Say what you want about me, but I'm not going to let you insult Jill."

"Then why is she here in my home?"

"I don't think you're getting it," I grit out. "She is done with you."

"Fine. Keep your slut."

Thank you for the invitation.

My fist connects with his jaw once, twice more, and the lights go out behind his eyes before he hits the ground.

That'll keep him down.

"Alex, your hand!"

Jill's wavering voice makes me drag my eyes away from Connor's form stirring at my feet. Blood smears my knuckles, and I don't think it's mine, but my middle finger sticks out at a sickening angle.

Dislocated. It's happened enough times in rugby games that I know what it looks like.

Worth it. If it wouldn't fuck up my hand more, I'd punch this waste of space again.

"What did you do?" a voice asks from behind me.

The blood thundering in my veins starts to slow and I look up to the circle of people around us, staring at me in shock and at Connor in disgust. Even his mother looks at him with revulsion.

With this many witnesses to what he said to her, I won't have a lawsuit on my hands.

"What someone should have done years ago," I say, tugging my finger to pop it back into its joint. *Jesus.* That's going to hurt like a bitch tomorrow.

Probably less than his face will hurt tomorrow.

I glare at Connor's friends, who haven't moved to help their friend to his feet. "Next time he runs his mouth like that in front of me, I won't be as forgiving," I warn, and receive a series of nods in return.

Good. They got the message.

I turn to the woman I love more than anything in the world. Jill looks like she's seconds away from slumping to the floor beside her piece of shit ex, or throwing up on him. I gently cup her face with both hands, making sure not to get his blood on her cheeks.

"I'm so sorry you had to see that."

That's a lie. I'm not sorry at all.

Now she knows she will never have to worry about me backing down from someone disrespecting her. That I will always be there to protect her.

And that she got to see Connor get a fraction of the beating he deserved.

The voices at our backs don't slow me down as I pull Jill through the house with one hand, the other ordering a cab. The only thing that stops me is when she doubles over at the waist, hands braced on her knees and gasping for air.

Fuck, it was too much. Her family. Connor. The violence. All of it together. No wonder she's having a panic attack. I sweep her up into my arms as I navigate the pathway out of the house and to our taxi.

Thank god the night is still early, and the cab is already pulling up to the long driveway as I reach the end of the walkway. I open the passenger door, and buckle her in.

"Jillian! Stop right now!"

Her parents jog down the path towards us, her mother's face twisted with displeasure, her father's etched with worry.

Now they come to check on her? After everything?

"Is she okay?" Arthur asks, face shiny with sweat. He tries to peer around me into the car.

"She's going to be—" I start, but Lizanne teeters to a stop at the edge of the walkway, fists dug into her waist.

"What do you think you are doing?" she hisses under her breath, as if someone back in the house might hear her. "There are a hundred people in that room that you abandoned."

I can't believe what I'm hearing. No concern for Jill. No apology for orchestrating this—because I'm sure it was her who made it possible for Connor to be here tonight. Just a worry that it might look poorly on her.

I don't give a fuck about making a good impression anymore.

Jill has shouldered her mother's expectations long enough. I stroke her cheek. "Stay here. I'll take care of you."

I carefully shut the taxi door and turn to my future in-laws.

"No. She's not okay. Her abusive ex-boyfriend insulted her in front of strangers. In a house that holds terrible memories for her, that you don't care about. You put her in a position to let it happen, and you haven't done a thing to protect her." I pause to scoop a handful of snow, hoping the cold will bring down my anger and swelling in my hand. It practically sizzles in my palm, and I draw a deep breath through clenched teeth. "Jill has struggled her entire life jumping through the hoops to make you two happy, and nothing is ever enough. And now you want to turn our wedding into some charade that is nothing like what she wants. On a day that is supposed to be all about her, you're making it all about you. So no, she's very far from okay."

In the wave of emotions that cross Lizanne's face, none of them are remorse. She presses her lips together, turns, and stalks back to the party without a word.

Her father pales, and his mouth opening and closing like a fish struggling to breathe in deoxygenated water. He looks helpless, lost. Who knows how many times he's been in the middle, loyalty divided between his wife and his daughter.

I have no sides to take. No divided loyalty. It's me and Jill facing life together. Even if what we face is her parents.

Arthur doesn't move, face to face with what the result of a lifetime of pressure has led to. Too late to see that now.

"I tried, Alex. I really did." His shoulders drop, his arms limp at his sides. "But you are taking better care of my little girl than I ever did," he says finally.

"I am." I turn my back on him and get into the waiting cab beside Jill. "And I'll do it for the rest of my life."

13

LINES

Months engaged: *almost ten*
Months until wedding: *twelve*

I SQUINT THROUGH THE GLARE CUTTING THROUGH OUR BEDROOM'S half-shuttered blinds. Slivers of bright, bluebird sky sneak between the slats, the barest glint of sun reflecting off the icicles growing from the eaves.

If it's this light, it has to be late. And Jill's still in bed with me.

In three years, she's slept in later than me exactly once. When Sophie came to visit, they stayed up until some ungodly hour and the pair woke up hungover just in time for lunch.

Now, even asleep, she looks tired. The dark circles under her eyes haven't cleared after our marathon return trip home the day before. Her leg is thrown across my hips, palm flat to my chest by her cheek. A small slick of drool has collected by her parted lips.

We skipped the hotel. No point in dragging out time. We hastily packed our things at her parents' place and went straight to the airport. The first flight back to Calgary left in the middle of the night. We shut off our phones, and Jill dozed in uncomfortable chairs until our flight left, then again on the flight home. I couldn't sleep. I watched her all night. I just had to know she was okay.

The flight attendant had the decency not to say anything when I asked him for a bag of ice for my hand.

I flex my fingers. Bruised and sore, but I'm fairly certain nothing is broken.

Should have hit that piece of shit one more time. Would have been worth breaking something.

I fumble for my phone and squint at the time. She's been sleeping for twelve hours straight.

I plant kisses on her eyelids until she stirs. "Morning, Jillybean."

"Morning." Her voice is a croaky rasp. "Happy birthday, Cupcake."

Right. With everything that happened, I've lost track of the days. "Waking up with you makes it a happy birthday already."

"Even when I'm drooling on you?"

"Especially when you're drooling on me."

Her snicker fades into a yawn. "What time is it?"

"Almost nine."

"I was going to make you breakfast in bed." Her eyes shut again. "I don't know why I'm so tired. Hope I didn't pick up a cold on the plane."

"No rush to get up." I ease the covers back. "Stay here."

I throw on a pair of boxes and stagger to the kitchen. I hum as I pour our coffee; black for her, and cream and sugar for me. I set the cup on her nightstand, and kiss her temple. "I love you," I say, smiling at the role reversal.

Jill grips the cup between her hands, propped back on the pillows and eyes still closed. A light grimace scrunches her nose. "Why does this smell weird?"

Maybe there's dish detergent on the mug? I sniff my cup. Normal. I take a whiff of hers. Nothing but the scent of strong coffee fills my nostrils. "Smells fine to me?"

"I think I need more sleep." Jill replaces her coffee on the nightstand and burrows back under the covers. "Spoon me?"

I'm not going to waste the opportunity. I almost never get this. Snuggling is my favourite thing to do in the morning. She's always up running somewhere. Often literally.

I slide my hand around her to cup her boob, pulling her in close and hunkering down for more sleep. She melts into me, soft and warm.

Really warm. Warmer than usual. The beat of her heart drums faster than usual, too. But she doesn't sound like she has a cold.

I snug my arm around her, flexing my fingers. Her breast feels different. Heavier? Fuller? My eyebrows draw together, and I switch my grip to her other breast.

Is she?

"Pretty sure they were both still there when I went to bed last night." Jill yawns through her sleepiness. "Ow! Be gentle."

They are indeed both there, but I've had my hands on her boobs every day for the past three years, and they don't feel like this.

And they are more sensitive than usual. Coffee is grossing her out. She's exhausted, even after a full night of sleep.

Every lingering cobweb of sleep vanishes in a flash.

Can it be happening already?

"Bean," I say, heart pounding against my ribs. "I think you should take a pregnancy test."

Her eyes snap open and she strips the covers off the bed. I'm right behind her as she rifles through the bathroom cabinet and rips open the pregnancy test.

It could be ...

She sits on the toilet, stick in hand, not moving, just looking at me.

"Don't you have to—"

"Alex," she whines. "I can't do it when you're standing here watching me."

Right. Tiny, shy bladder. "Okay. I'll just …"

Wait outside and listen to you pee from the hall.

I cross my arms, uncross them, and cross them again, bruised fingers drumming on my biceps. I hover outside the door, head tucked, and burst in the moment she calls me in.

"Well?" I say, rocking on the balls of my feet.

Jill sets the test on the counter, facing away from us. She perches on the edge of the bathtub and clasps her hands between her thighs, knees bouncing. A nervous smile lifts the corner of her mouth. "It's ready in three minutes."

I race back to the bedroom to grab my phone to set the timer. I drop my phone beside the test and sit beside Jill.

"We're probably not …" I start.

"We've only been trying for a month."

"Most people take a while."

"A year."

"Or longer."

Jill glances at the test, her hands on her belly. I scoop her into my lap, and we watch the phone's timer tick down.

It's the longest three minutes of my life.

The timer goes off like a firecracker, and we bolt to our feet.

"Ready?"

"On the count of three."

"One, two, three."

Jill turns the test over, and space dissolves.

"Alex," she says, her eyes shining as she holds up the test.

Bright, undeniably, unmistakably blue. Two lines. Marking a clear path to our future.

It's happening. This is really happening.

I lunge forward to crush her into a hug as a giddy laugh rips from my throat and echoes off the bathroom tiles. "We're going to have a baby!"

Jill's own shriek matches mine, and she wraps her legs around my waist.

"Put me down! I'm going to barf." Jill's laugh fills the room, and she disentangles her legs. I wind my hands into her hair, tilting her face to mine. My thumbs wipe the happy tears from her cheeks as our lips meet.

Messy hair, flushed skin. She's more beautiful than I've ever seen her. My hand drifts to where her hand hovers over her flat belly.

A belly that will spend the next nine months growing our child.

Holy shit.

We're going to have a baby.

I'm going to be a father.

My entire world tilts and recentres around a new axis as my knees go weak, and suddenly, life as I knew it is forever changed. All the words I've been holding in for a year spill out.

"I don't want to wait another year to get married," I say in a rush. "I want you to be my wife before our baby is born. I want you to have my name and be Mrs. Campbell. I want to get married here."

Jill's mouth opens in surprise. Her chest is still heaving, eyes slightly dazed. "Why didn't you say this sooner?"

"I just want to make you happy. And if that means a perfect wedding, with the dress and the flowers and the, I don't know, purple tablecloths or whatever, we can wait." I get on my knees and cover her hands in mine. "But I just want you to be my wife."

A shadow crosses her face. "My parents—"

"Don't get to dictate what we do with our lives. And if they are worried about money, I spent more on lab equipment last month than they sunk into deposits. I'll pay them back. But this?" I brush a strand of hair away from her cheek and rub my thumb over her lips. "You bending over backwards for your mother? Guest lists full of people we don't love and a dress you don't want? This isn't healthy for you. And it's not what we want."

Jill picks the pregnancy test again, her breath coming out in a rush. "You're right. It's not what we want. It hasn't been from the start." She looks up to me, eyes sparkling. "I have an idea."

Days married: *one*

It's funny how fast things come together when Jill can do what she wants.

We don't bother with decorations. No worries about tablecloths or centrepieces. A cryptic note invites our friends to a casual get-together the following week. The only ask is to bring food and folding chairs and be ready to hang out in our backyard. It's a testament to the hardiness of our friends that no one blinks an eye that we'll be outside in January. After dinner and under blankets, forty people scream when I announce we are getting married.

The night is a gorgeous blur. Gemma cries when she braids the ivory ribbon into Jill's hair. I can barely remember what we said in our vows, but it ended with *I do* and kissing each other in front of everyone we love.

And that was all I wanted from the start.

"Congrats, Doc." Dan chucks me on the arm. His daughter is draped over his shoulder, icing from our grocery store wedding cake smeared on her cheek.

His girlfriend leans in for a hug and adjusts the swaddle on their new son. He's so small, his tiny pumpkin of a head nearly buried under his cap. "Sorry we have to duck out early," she says. "This little guy's going to get cranky if we don't get home soon."

That's going to be us, this time next year. I can't wait.

At the same time, I want time to slow down. To watch her grow. To savour every minute, every second, while no one knows this secret but the two of us.

And Sophie. She guessed the minute we picked her up from

the airport last night. She's already angling for us to name the baby after her, if it's a girl.

I peer past Dan to where Jill sits with Cass and Libby. "I'll get Jill to come and say good-bye."

I walk into the conversation with Cass wiping fresh tears from her eyes and Libby grinning from ear-to-ear.

"You sneak," Libby says, elbowing Jill in the ribs. "Wedding planning apps weren't cutting it for you?"

I grit my teeth, and force myself not to bat Libby's elbow away.

Relax. A friendly ribbing won't hurt Jill or the baby.

"Couldn't decide on the tablecloths." I say, butting into the conversation. "Pardon me, but I need to steal my wife."

My wife. I wonder when saying the words will stop making me dizzy.

Jill looks up at me with such a soft expression my bones weaken. She puts her hand in mine and lets me pull her to her feet. "Okay, husband."

A grin splits my face. I know I'll never get tired of hearing that.

Sophie sidles over. "I'll run interference and shut things down tonight. You two get out of here."

I don't need to be told twice to take my wife to bed.

Jill sags in gratitude. "You're the best, Soph."

"I know."

I lead Jill through our house, to our bedroom, and take her hands in mine. "You doing okay?" I ask.

"I keep reading about how exhausting the first trimester is," Jill says, hiding a yawn behind her hand. "I think this is just the beginning."

When we make love for the first time as husband and wife, it's slow and quiet. And after, I rest my palm on the dip of her belly, the gold band on my ring finger gleaming.

There's still so much to do. We don't have a new house yet. Or a nursery. A mountain of work waits for me.

But we're here. Together. In a way perfect for us.
Jill is right. It's just the beginning.

ACKNOWLEDGMENTS

The epilogue wasn't supposed to be this long.

This was supposed to be a one-shot (pun absolutely intended) to give Connor what he deserved. And then I got into Alex's brain and I didn't want to leave.

So many people had eyes on this along the way. Marlee, thank you for reviewing in the very beginning when the last chapter consisted of a single sentence ending with a question mark. Alex, you helped me dial back some of the diabetes. Yes, I know I put some of it right back in. Cece, Riya, and Luna, thanks for helping me figure out bench logistics. Thank you all for putting up with my endless cream pie jokes in the chat.

Kelsey, your final parting comment let me know I hit the tone I was going for. Thank you!!

To my street team! Thank you for your hyping and sharing and unhinged DMs when you were reading ahead of everyone else. A, Annie, Beckie & Jamie, Harp, Hrishika, Iesha, Maéva, and Tru - I am so grateful!!

The Literary Poutine Posse. Thank you to this group of cheer-leading baddies who are generous with ideas and support.

Mr. Douglas, I kept that line you wanted. I'm sorry I didn't include any Fokker triplanes. Maybe next time. Your love and encouragement is everything. I love you.

ALSO BY ELLORY DOUGLAS

A Bluebird Sky Series

Book 1 - A Better Proposal

Book 2 - A Lucky Shot

Book 3 - 2025

Stay up to date with upcoming works by signing up for my quarterly newsletter at www.ellorydouglas.ca

Want a sneak peek into book three? Turn the page!

Up until three years ago, Nick Martin had everything. A successful startup poised to go unicorn. A best friend and business partner to run it with. A rotation of women to call at his whim. Then, one—admittedly bad—decision turned everything to high-grade fertilizer.

NICK'S STORY
COMING 2025

Excerpt is unedited and subject to change.

Chloé trudged through the front door and let out a jaw-splitting yawn. "I'm going to bed."

Nick trailed after her and into the narrow hallway, dodging her kicked-off shoes and discarded jacket from the entryway tiles. "Or you could take five seconds to put your things away."

Before you leave me to take care of it. Again.

"Tomorrow." Chloé dumped her suitcase in the middle of the living room and cracked open a soda from the fridge, swigging straight from the can as she rifled through the cupboards. "Jet lag. I need my beauty sleep."

"People don't get jet lag from two hour time differences."

"I do." She tore open a bag of chips, scattering crumbs on the counter, and let out a low burp as she brushed past him.

Nick eyed the half-empty can left on the counter. "I suppose you aren't thirsty anymore."

"You can have it," she replied, calling over her shoulder as she disappeared into her bedroom.

Trust his baby sister to turn their place into a pig sty in under two minutes.

Fine. It wasn't too late. A bit of caffeine wouldn't affect his sleep. Going to bed with a messy apartment would. He tidied the mess she left behind, poured the rest of the soda into a glass, and plunked himself on the couch.

> we're here

> you'll be shocked when I tell you Chloé coded a new game on her phone on the flight over

> I have never been less shocked

> you doing okay?

> Thanks Nico. I'm holding up.

> Miss you two already.

> miss you too, Laur

Today was always a hard day. For him and Laurence, anyway. Chloé was too young to remember her.

Doomscrolling might keep him up, even if the extra caffeine wouldn't, but the flight and memories left him too wired to go to sleep. He sipped the soda, trying to think of who to look up, but the first person who came to mind would be the last to reply.

Yo, Alex, my man! What's new? How's the company? How are your nephews? Still dating Jill?

Still want to shove me through a wall and stomp my face in?

Two and a half years later, the answer to that question likely hadn't changed.

Why would it have? He'd gone behind the back of his business partner—his best friend—and changed a government funding application. The changes hadn't been *wrong*. Just … optimistic.

And premature. And unnecessary.

It cost him his best friend.

He'd been a goddamn fool. For nothing.

Nick chugged the last of the soda and bent his head to his phone. A quick search proved what he already suspected: Alex still didn't have any social media.

Cass. He could always text her. Things were simple between them. Just being around her made him feel good. They didn't even need to talk.

The last time he saw her was last fall. Or was it summer? The contract he was working had only been a few days, and his flight back to Montreal had him leaving the next morning. He grimaced, remembering his weak reply to her good morning text. No wonder she had blown him off the next time he texted her.

He swiped through her recent photos. Cass always looked gorgeous, but her new profile picture was *phenomenal*, like it belonged in an art gallery. There was something about her expression, playful and open. She'd never smiled at him like that. He took a screenshot and kept scrolling.

The first few photos on her grid were on soundstages, all captions with versions of *you won't believe what's coming #sd*. He thumbed the angle of his jaw in thought. She had mentioned she worked in some artistic field. Theatre? TV? That would make sense. He creeped back through her timeline.

The candid shot was taken at night. Alex's arms were wrapped around Jill, who grinned at something out of frame. His backyard, too. Nick checked the date: Alex's birthday. A look of absolute bliss radiated from him, his eyes closed and lips on her cheek. It was the happiest Nick had ever seen him.

He swiped to a second photo. The two of them were kissing. Or trying too—they were laughing too hard to properly press their lips together—while a small crowd of people behind them cheered. More photos, some with people he knew; others, he didn't. He swiped again, and landed on a photo that spread a smile across his face.

I guess you aren't dating Jill anymore.

Congratulations to these two sneaks, the photo's caption read.

Being here with you two making it official is almost enough to make me forgive you for getting married outside in January. So grateful to share your day!!

Alex, his best friend, had gotten married. Without him. Not that he would have expected an invite, but …

But what *did* he expect? Of course he wasn't invited. That part of his life was over. And it was his fault.

A notification popped up on Cass's page. She'd been tagged in a video.

Curious, Nick tapped on the link.

Holy shit. Some local influencer's green screened head floated over a shot of a couple. The footage was blurry, but there was no mistaking Cass.

With a celebrity.

More things had changed than he could have imagined. He opened his messages and hammered out a note.

> are you dating dawson james??

How do you know about Dawson?

> So you are??

> you were tagged in a video

> Kissing, it looked like

D and I are just friends

Nick let out a sigh of relief. He and Cass were friends who kissed, even if it wasn't as often as they used to.

Frankly, he'd missed her, and not just what that mouth could do. Cass had always said they had a good time together. Good enough that she'd suggested once or twice that they should make it a regular thing.

Their timing had always been terrible. But now?

He was back in town. He could find out what she wanted from him. Maybe catch him up on what else had changed in the last couple of years. A twinge of guilt squirmed in his stomach. If he remembered correctly, they hadn't talked much last time they hung out.

Nick glanced at the bedroom door, shut tight. Chloé slept like the dead. No chance she'd wake up before tomorrow morning. She didn't need *that* much of a babysitter. If he slipped out for a few hours, she'd never know.

He scrolled through a few more photos in Cass's feed. She looked good. Damn good.

It would be nice to feel good again.

> Not sad to hear that ;)
>
> You looked beautiful as usual
>
> Wyd now?

It's late. I'm almost in bed

He deleted his first reply: *I've got a bed you can spend some time in*. Not with Chloé here. And that wasn't what he wanted.

Not all of what he wanted, anyway.

> please
>
> I'd really like to see you

The bubbles disappeared and danced for so long he almost put his phone away.

okay

A wave of relief washed over him. Maybe he hadn't fucked everything up.

He'd fucked everything up.

Nick stared at her back as she left the coffee shop, with her head held high and shoulders back. Cass was done with him. For real this time.

You've had so many chances to show me you care, but you treated me like something you could ignore until I was convenient. I'm worth more than being someone's second choice, and I don't want to ever have to guess if I am again. If you've changed, I'm glad. And I hope the next person you claim to care about gets a better version of you than what you gave me.

Her words didn't change, no matter how many times he replayed them in his head, sitting with a cooling coffee when he thought they'd be on their way back to her place already. Even if it was just to talk.

Preferably to talk, for once. He didn't have anyone for that.

His fingers itched to open up his phone and find someone else. It was the easy thing to do. Just find some pussy and blow off some steam. But Cass was right. He had treated everyone like shit. Like they were temporary.

He told her he'd changed, but how? He'd never done anything to show her. Now he'd never have the chance.

She said she hoped the next person he claimed to care about got a better version of him.

And he had no idea what a better version of him was.

ABOUT THE AUTHOR

Ellory loves cinnamon roll book boyfriends, everything pink, and summer evenings on the patio with her husband and a glass of wine. She lives, works, and writes wholesome, horny, happily-ever-afters in and about Calgary, Canada. You can usually find her outside, even when it's -30 C.

- instagram.com/authorellorydouglas
- goodreads.com/ellorydouglas

Manufactured by Amazon.ca
Acheson, AB

14581953R00076